Th  Man
Book 1: Pulse

As always – to my wife, Polly and my son, Axel. You chase the shadows from my soul.

Once I said to a scarecrow, "You must be tired of standing in this lonely field."

And he said, "The joy of scaring is a deep and lasting one, and I never tire of it."

Said I, after a minute of thought, "It is true; for I too have known that joy."

Said he, "Only those who are stuffed with straw can know it."

Then I left him, not knowing whether he had complimented or belittled me.

Kahli Gibran

Chapter 1

Master Gunnery Sergeant Nathaniel Hogan stood outside the new American embassy at Nine Elms, London and stared at the boats drifting down the river Thames. He was dressed in his standard combat utility uniform or 'digies', so called because of their MARPAT Digital camouflage. He was wearing the darker woodland version as opposed to the light desert one, even though, strictly speaking, it was for winter use only.

Hogan was a large man. Raw boned, six foot four, around two hundred and forty pounds. And, at only twenty-six years old, one of the youngest Master Gunnery Sergeants in the corp. His black hair was cut in the standard Marine style, short back and sides, the length not exceeding three inches. He was clean-shaven. His eyes, deep set under thick eyebrows, their dark green color like emeralds in pools of shadow. High cheekbones suggested Native American ancestry backed up by his broad, white teeth and straight Roman nose.

He did not carry an assault rifle but, on his hip rode a Colt 1911M25, the latest update of the venerable 1911. Still chambered for the 45 cal round but with a staggered magazine holding ten rounds and also with an inbuilt compensator.

He glanced at his watch. Eighteen hundred hours. The last of the public had left. Sunset was forecast for twenty hundred. Change of guard was scheduled for the same time.

Hogan was in charge of eight Marines stationed at the embassy. It was what the corps called a 'reward posting'. Eighteen months of cushy duty in one of the most fun cities in the world. Tonight he was knocking off after change of guard and was heading into the city to meet an English girl. Emma Rittington. Tall, blonde, horse rider's build. His English friends referred to her as Posh Totty, his American ones said that she was 'Fancy.' She had a three-bed apartment, or flat, in Sloane Square and seemed to want for nothing. But that was not what attracted the Marine sergeant to her. His attraction to her was based almost entirely on the physical. In all fairness, she had admitted to the same about him. Plus, being an American and a non-commissioned officer had, in her words, 'caused daddy a veritable lavatory full of anguish', something that seemed to give her an inordinate amount of pleasure.

He gazed once more at the Thames. The clouds in the sky reflected in the fast flowing water below, a brown mottled facsimile of the firmament above.

And then a rainbow of color skittered across the surface. Like a thousand gallons of oil had been instantly dumped into the water. An orgasm of color. Hogan glanced up to see the sky ablaze with light. Flowing forward, retreating, spreading and coalescing. He had seen this sight before, although never with such clarity. And never in broad sunlight. He had seen it when he had been seconded to the embassy in Moscow. It was the Aurora Borealis or Northern Lights. He stared at it, entranced, as it rippled across the sky. Vast. Overpowering. And utterly silent. With such a vast display he expected some sort of accompanying sound. Thunder. Wind. Some sort of environmental drum roll. But nothing. Not a sound.

He cocked his head to one side and concentrated. The silence was eerie. In fact, there was no sound. Nothing at all. The constant background of a city in motion was not there.

Two and a half million cars and buses. Two thousand eight hundred construction sites, one thousand road working projects, one hundred and twenty thousand air-conditioning units, over one hundred passenger carrying commercial aircraft.

Silent.

Then the sound of running footsteps. Marine corporal Manson sprinted up and came to attention in front of him.

'Master Guns, the power in the building is out and the emergency generator hasn't cut in. Complete power failure.'

'Right, Manson. Tell the men to stay at their posts. Then find the janitor and see what you can do with the generator. Double time.'

Manson didn't move. It was as though he had been frozen in place, staring with wide eyes over Hogan's shoulder. And then, like a man pointing at his own death, he raised an arm. Hogan turned to look.

The sky was raining aircraft. Ten, twenty, thirty of them. Thousands of tons of steel plummeting down from the skies. Spinning clumsily to earth. Succumbing to the laws of gravity that had hereto been conquered by three hundred thousand horsepower jet engines.

The first one struck the city. Kensington. Dust, then flame. Finally, sound. A massive thumping wall of sound as the one hundred thousand liters of aviation fuel exploded.

Within seconds the next aircraft plowed in. And the next. And the next.

Brentford, Fulham, Shepherd's Bush. Belgravia.

The sounds of the explosions thundered through the city. But there was no corresponding sound of sirens. No klaxons of fire engines. No warning bells. Nothing but the sound of fire. They were too far away to hear the screams of the dying.

Hogan grabbed the corporal by his shoulder and shook hard. 'Manson. Ten-hut. Now, go inside. Tell the civvies to stay indoors. Get sergeant Johnson to open the armory. I want all Marines in full battle gear, M16s, four extra mags, colts, two extra mags. Bring me my gear plus a M249M22 machine gun plus three 200 round belts with bags. Move.'

Training took over rational thought and Manson sprinted off, heading back into the embassy.

Hogan trotted across to the main gates. On the way he pulled his cell phone out and looked at the screen. Dead.

The two Marines there came to attention. Faces ashen with shock, but discipline still intact.

'Ronaldo. Jessup.'

'Master sergeant,' asked PFC Ronaldo. 'What's happening?'

'Can't be sure, Marine. I suspect an EMP strike. Some sort of electromagnetic pulse.'

'Are we under attack, Master Guns?'

Hogan thought for a few seconds. 'Remains to be seen, soldier. Could be natural causes. Could be a nuclear detonation in the atmosphere. Johnson and Manson are tooling up, they'll bring your kit. I want you all in full battle gear. Stay at your posts. I'll be back.'

Hogan strode back towards the embassy doors. Halfway there, Johnson and Manson came jogging out, festooned with armfuls of kit. Johnson carried on to the men at the gate. Manson helped Hogan on with his kit. Modern tactical vest with scalable armor plates. Camelbak hydration pack complete with inline water purification system. First aid kit. Enhanced combat helmets. Ammunition carrying vest with extra ammunition bags attached. And finally, the M249M22 light machine gun.

'Master Guns,' said Manson. 'I ran into the sparky. He said that the generator is FU. Circuits all burnt out.'

Hogan knelt down and placed the butt of

the M249M22 on his knee, wracked the charging handle, released the feed tray cover and clipped in a belt of ammo. As he stood up he saw Liz Tutor, the Deputy Chief of Mission, approaching. She descended the stairs rapidly. Low heeled sensible shoes. Calf length skirt. Brown bob as sleek and hard as a helmet. Teeth as white as a Hollywood wanabee.

'Master Guns.'

'Ma'am.'

'What is going on?'

'Looks like some sort of EMP strike, ma'am. An electrical pulse that seems to have taken out all of our electronic capabilities. The generator has burnt out, all comms are down and aircraft are falling out of the sky. I have put the Marines on full alert.'

'Are we under attack?'

'Not enough intel, ma'am. But if I had to guess I'd say that it's a natural occurrence.' Hogan pointed at the sky. 'Aurora Borealis, ma'am. If it were a nuke then the sky would be clear.'

'So, what do we do now?'

'Not sure, ma'am. Perhaps we should ask the ambassador.'

'Can't. He's not here today. Meeting with the British PM.'

'Well then, ma'am, I suggest that we batten down the hatches and wait a while. See what transpires. Keep everyone indoors; we have enough food and water for at least ten days. I'll get one of the boys to break out the gas lamps and cookers. Tomorrow we see what happens and react accordingly.'

Liz nodded her approval. 'How long before help comes?' She asked.

Hogan took a deep breath. 'Ma'am, there will be no help. Particularly if this has been a worldwide phenomenon. No transport, no comms. We're on our own, ma'am.'

Liz shook her head. 'Don't be silly, Master Guns. We are Americans, the most powerful nation on the face of the planet. I hardly think that a mere power outage is going to bring us to our knees. However, I accept that we stay here tonight. I am sure that we shall hear good news by tomorrow.'

She turned and clipped back up the stairs into the embassy.

Hogan went and stood by the gate next to the two other Marines.

The sun sank slowly behind the horizon.

And London glowed with fire. Every now and then the still night was rocked with an explosion as a fuel station or gas line erupted, sending vast balls of flame heavenwards.

And as the night progressed, the two thousand year old city began to burn its way back into the dark ages.

But what humanity did not yet know was that the pulse was not only affecting earth. It was also calling. Across unimaginable distances measured in both time and dimension.

The Pulse had called.

And something had heard.

***

Commander Ammon Set-Bat of the Fair-Folk stood outside his flag tent and looked up at the sky. It was dull. Blue and ugly without its usual wash of psychedelic colors pulsing through it. There was barely the vaguest hint of the Life-Light at all. Maybe a tiny coruscation on the horizon. But then that may have been wishful thinking, admitted Ammon to himself. For without the Life-Light in the skies the Fair-Folk had nowhere to draw their power from. Their magik was useless without the powers of the lights. Weak and insubstantial. If they were to survive then they would need to follow the Life-Light to another place where it was strong and enduring. And there they would prosper. The Fair-Folk had done this before, many, many times throughout their ancient history

Where the Life-Light went, so did they.

But in all fairness, said Ammon to himself, there was little chance of that happening and, even if it did, there was even less chance that his people would survive the ongoing war that they were in. Perhaps this was the end.

No! He took a deep breath, brought his attention back to the moment and continued to survey the valley below. He had no use for a telescope as he had long since perfected the art of 'Farlooking' and could identify a species of butterfly at a distance of over half a league.

As the commander of the army, Ammon was a member of the Council of Twelve that ruled the Fair-Folk and their minions and, at the moment, his army had been stretched across the narrow part of the valley of Southee. On each side of the Vale rose the Sethanon Mountains, a natural redoubt between the High Kingdom and the Midlands. This valley was the only practical way through. So here he had placed his troops.

Five battalions of Orcs totaling one hundred thousand strong. Six thousand heavy armored Trolls with their twenty-foot pikes and massive shields. The Trolls would provide a wall of armor that he hoped the enemy would break against like a tide against a cliff. To the rear, forty thousand Goblin archers, their small-recurved bows already strung, bundles of arrows at their feet.

And finally, the Constructs, noticeable by their shining white tunics and slow behavior. These ever-smiling, pale skinned creations of the Fair-Folk would carry water, bandages and extra arrows to the combatants. Afterwards, if there was an afterwards, they would be used by the Orcs and goblins for their more…comely offerings.

There were no Fair-Folk in the battle formation. Their talents lay in ruling, creating, commanding, controlling. Not for them the savage cruelty of front line combat. And even if they had wanted to participate in a more physical way they could not have made much difference.

The males stood around four feet tall, hairless smooth gray skin, no discernable musculature, massive dome shaped heads, no perceivable ears or nostrils, small mouths and large black eyes. Their bodies merely an ambulatory system for their extraordinarily advanced brains. Brains capable of controlling those lesser than them, capable of psychokinesis, pyrokinesis and, most importantly, harnessing the power of the 'Life-Light'. Although, as Ammon had been musing, in recent years, the Life-Light had been fading, its power waning. And with it, the power of the Fair-Folk.

The female of the species was seldom seen. Smaller and much lighter skinned than the male with smaller elongated heads. They were kept indoors, away from the sunlight and, when they did wish to venture outside they were transported in curtained palanquins or sedan chairs carried by two battle Orcs.

Like the males, the females lived for well over three hundred years, during which time they usually laid three or four embryonic sacs. These sacs were fertilized by the males who squatted over them and sprayed them with their seed. The Fair-Folks' pleasures were far more esoteric than mere sex, something that they deemed suitable only for the lower ranks of beings.

Today marked the end of a year of continual war. A year of constant, bitter failure as, yard-by-yard, the alien Elvish had conquered the Fair-Folks' kingdom. Forcing them back by virtue of numbers. They were no more than acceptable combatants, tall and almos
unbelievably slim with heart shaped faces, flaxen hair as fine as cobwebs and small pointed teeth. But their numbers combined

with their hive-mentality made them a formidable foe. Their battle strategies were poor but, due to the fact that their minds were linked via the hive-queen, their reactions as a group were uncanny. Breaches in their lines were filled immediately, replacements always arrived at the perfect moment and supplies were always delivered at the exact time needed. They never panicked; they seldom fell for any subterfuge or ruse and their morale stayed at a constant high as they drew strength from the queen.

Ammon exerted his Far-looking powers and saw them coming. A murky amorphous mass of warriors, dressed in their customary dark green. Moving as one, like a shoal of fish, or flock of birds.

They had first appeared, a year before, in the Lower kingdoms. There had been a period of solar upheaval, days had shortened, nights had grown colder and the constant sky glow of the Life-Light had ceased for almost six days.

Then a hole had opened. A literal doorway, albeit a huge one, between the kingdoms and the godforsaken place that the Elvish came from. They had poured through the gap, taking the majority of the coastal towns of the Eastern Lower Kingdom in a matter of days.

Ammon had assembled his troops and force-marched from the highlands to meet the host on the Midland plains. He had quickly learned not to fight the Elven hordes in huge set battles. Their numbers were too large and their hive-minds ensured that their mass maneuvers were always perfect.

So instead he had fought a hundred smaller battles, always picking his ground with great care. Mountain passes, river confluences, forests. Anything to stop his dwindling army from being enveloped by the vast numbers of enemy.

And, as the year had gone by, the rainbow flickering of the Life-Light had grown dimmer in the skies. In the time-before it used to coruscate across the heavens, a constant surge of color, like lamp oil spilt on water, bringing with it the power that the Fair-Folk used to drive their magiks. The raw power of the universe. The power of the Life-Light.

He sensed rather than heard Seth Hil-Nu walk up to his side. Seth was the paramount mage of the Fair-Folk and he, more than any others, had been diminished by the dying of the Life-Light, his magnificent powers waning day by day. In the times-before, when the Life-Light was strong, he could have conjured up a raft of fireballs that would have burned the Elven host from the valley. He could have brought the mountains down on them or caused a storm of lightning to blast them from existence. Now he was simply a source of wisdom, capable of the odd small magik if the circumstances were right.

'Well seen, Seth,' greeted the commander.

'Well met, Ammon. How long before battle commences?'

'Mere minutes, mage. Mere minutes. Pray tell, can you amplify my voice so that the troops can hear me? I used to be able to do it myself when the Life-Light was strong, but now it is a skill that escapes me.'

'Sad are the times when you have to ask if I can still perform such tiny magiks,' answered Seth. 'But yes, I can make you heard. Not through amplification, but they will hear what you say.'

'Thank you, mage.'

The Elven swarm continued to pour into the valley, running on fast lithe feet. Drawing closer.

Ammon waited and then, 'Archers, make ready.'

The four thousand goblins each lent forward, picked up a dozen or so arrows and planted them, head down, in the turf in front of them, ready for rapid fire.

'Archers, string.'

Four thousand arrows were notched.

'Draw.'

Four thousand bow strings thrummed with tension as the archers drew to full draw and held.

'Rapid fire, now!'

The average competent goblin archer can unleash an arrow every three seconds. The flight time from archer to target was approximately nine seconds. This meant that, by the time the first four thousand arrows struck, there were already another twelve thousand in the air. Like a swarm of steel tipped locusts, blotting out the sun.

They struck the Elvin ranks with a sound like hail hitting a cornfield. A thudding and tearing as they punctured flesh and bone. But still the horde ran on, climbing over their dead as they did so.

Ammon waited until the foes were almost too close for the archers to safely fire at without risking hitting their own troops.

'Archers – cease-fire. Trolls, prepare.'

The six hundred Trolls stepped forward, each standing over twelve foot tall, weighing in at over nine hundred pounds, ten foot high shields of steel and twenty foot long pikes with massive broad blades. They locked their shields together with a mighty clash of steel that reverberated around the valley. Pikes were held over the interlocked shields.

'Trolls, advance.'

Over five hundred tons of heavily armored muscle shambled forward. Trolls did not, could not, run. Instead they shuffled, feet never leaving the ground. As a result they were always solidly grounded. In an advance such as this, nothing could stand before them.

A solid wall of sound rolled across the valley as the Trolls crashed into the lightweight Elves. Pikes rose and fell, slicing, cutting, destroying. And slowly, ever so slowly, the Elven hoard was pushed back.

But not for long. The sheer weight of numbers eventually slowed the advance and then halted it.

Ammon was ready for this.

'Orcs, support the advance.'

The twenty five thousand Orcs ran forward. Not unsheathing their battle-axes. Instead they simply ran into the Trolls, dropping their shoulders and pushing. The Trolls pikes continued to rise and fall, slashing a pathway through the horde. The extra power of the Orcs continued the advance, driving the Elves back, crushing them underfoot, compacting them together so tightly that they could no longer wield their weapons.

Then, with the timing brought from years of experience, Ammon spoke his next command.

'Orcs, unsheath your weapons. Trolls, unlock your shields. Orcs – attack.'

Twenty five thousand Orc voices bayed their battle cry as they ran forward through the ranks of the Trolls and into the massed Elves, two-handed battle-swords swinging with abandon, the battle madness on them all.

'Kamateh,' they cried out their war cry as they hacked and killed.

'Kamateh, kill, kill them all!'

The Elven horde broke and ran. Darting away like a massive shoal of bait fish before a pack of sharks.

And commander Ammon gave his last order. 'Archers, harry them. Fire at will.'

The Elves retreated under a rain of steel tipped death.

Chapter 2

His name was Kobus Pistorious. He was fifty-four years old and he had emigrated from South Africa to England some twenty years previously. For the bulk of his life Kobus had been a mercenary in Africa. From Angola to Zanzibar. He had fought in over seventeen conflicts and as a result he was rabid racist and anti-communist. He was also a very good soldier.

Now he had semi-retired. He ran an online company that sold pet toys to the type of English person that talked to their pet and fed it at the table. Kobus was not that type of person. But one had to make a living.

When the pulse hit he was driving home from a dentist appointment and was just outside the cathedral city of Canterbury. He was waiting at a level crossing when his car cut out. He tried to restart it but it was totally dead. Not a spark.

He pulled the bonnet ratchet and stepped out of the car. The first thing that struck him was the silence. Not the silence of the grave but a comparative silence. The silence of the bush. Something that he had not heard since his days in Africa. The silence of a land without modern civilization. No cars, no radios, no horns honking.

Kobus had worked with special force units before. British SAS, American Rangers. And they had discussed this exact scenario. So, his first assumption was very close to correct: an EMP.

His second assumption was incorrect, but essentially it made little difference to his reaction.

'The bloody communists,' he said out loud. 'They've just gone and bleeding nuked us.'

He went to the rear of his car, opened the trunk, took out his double barrel shotgun and loaded it with buckshot. Then he stuffed a few extra rounds into his pockets, picked up an empty tog-bag and headed for the nearest drug store that happened to be just around the corner.

He opened the door and walked in. It was dark, especially near the back where the prescriptions were filled out. He strode down to the rear and threw the tog-bag onto the counter.

'Fill that up with broad-spectrum antibiotics, oral and intravenous. Also one hundred 25-gauge needles and one hundred ten mil disposable syringes. If there's any space left fill it with painkillers. Real ones with codeine, not aspirin or crap like that.'The pharmacist stared at Kobus, his mouth open.

'I'm sorry, sir, but that's impossible. You'll need some sort of prescription or…'

The South African raised the shotgun up and pulled the trigger. The light fitting above the pharmacist's head exploded into a thousand tiny shards.

'There's my bloody prescription. Now fill it.'

The pharmacist, face as pale as death, started to stuff boxes into the tog-bag with shaking hands. His assistant, a middle aged lady who had been standing behind him now lay on the floor, her hands covering her head, whimpering.

Kobus replaced the used shotgun cartridge, his hands moving quickly and assuredly. Doing something that they did well.

As soon as the bag was full Kobus ran from the drugstore, heading for the local cash and carry food store that was on his way home.

He slung the bag over his shoulder as he barreled into the food store, grabbing a large shopping trolley as he did.

A young colored man behind the till called out.

'Hey, man, sorry but the power's out. Till's not working so we can't allow any shopping. Sorry, mate. Should be back on soon if you'd like to wait.'

Kobus turned to face the man, bringing the shotgun to bear as he did so. The young man shrank back.

'Listen, Sambo,' said Kobus. 'Firstly, the lights are never coming back on and secondly, I'm not shopping, I'm helping myself. Now keep your cheeky black African face out of mine and maybe I won't kill you.'

The young man, whose name was actually Charles, born and bred in Kent, England and never having been within six thousand miles of Africa, simply said nothing. His face a blank mask.

Kobus ran down the aisles filling the trolley with tins of meat, vegetables and bottled water. When it was full he walked out the front door, pushing the squeaking trolley in front of him.

He was feeling good. Exultant even. For once he was truly ahead of the game. Drugs, food, a weapon. Happy days.

He didn't even hear Charles walk up behind him but, at the very last moment some sixth sense flashed a warning and he started to turn.

It was too late. The Niblick wedge golf club with the steel shaft and the dual reinforced bar at the back, struck the South African directly on the temple, smashing his skull and killing him before he struck the ground. He collapsed in an untidy heap on the sidewalk.

Charles stared at the body, aghast at what he had just done. Frantically he scrabbled for his cell phone to dial 999. But there was no signal. And there never would be. Ever again.

Kobus Pistorious was the first person, post pulse, to have been killed for looting. But his name would not go down in history. In fact no one would remember him. Not even Charles who died three days later defending his shop from a mob of looters.

A new history had begun.

Chapter 3

PULSE Plus 10 minutes 28th August 2022

United States of America
Airline crashes – 400 000 dead
Collateral damage from crashes – 180 000 dead
Patients in operating theatres – 25 000 dead
Patients on life support – 1 400 dead
Vehicle and train accidents – 18 000 dead
Other – 12 000 dead
TOTAL DEATHS USA – 636 400

United Kingdom
Airline crashes – 80 000 dead
Collateral damage from crashes – 120 000 dead
Patients in operating theatres – 5 000 dead
Patients on life support – 300 dead
Vehicle and train accidents – 8 000 dead
Other – 2 000 dead
TOTAL DEATHS UK – 215 300

Kamua Johnson had turned nine last week. He lived on the twenty-second floor of the Lambeth Towers development. A Thirty-story, horseshoe shaped tenement block that overlooked the sprawl of Brixton. Designed in the sixties as part of England's Brave New World policy. Blue plywood window surrounds, bare concrete. Planters on the ground floor complete with stringy trees, withered from pollution and lack of nutrients.

The original artist's impressions had shown lithe figures pushing buggies, playing ball, skipping rope. White, Asian, African. Shaded by tall Plane trees, the ground covered in freshly mown green lawn. The figures were smiling. All of them.

The reality was a crumbling urban nightmare of damp and decay. Disintegrating concrete, bare earth, puddles of rank water that never drained away. A pile of broken shopping trolleys. Without wheels. Twisted and crippled. Teenagers in hoodies. Hands in pockets. No one smiled. None of them.

Kamua shared the apartment with his parents and his grandmother, Gramma Johnson. His parents in one room, Gramma in the other. He slept in the sitting room.

Gramma suffered from Dementia or Alzheimer's disease. She was also a type 1 diabetes sufferer. But as long as she took her pills and her insulin injections she was manageable.

The problem was that Kamua's mother administered Gramma's drugs and neither she nor her husband had come home last night. Kamua had tried to phone her work, using the emergency number that she had left, scrawled on the yellow post-it and stuck to the mirror in the hallway. But the phones were dead. Both the landline and the cell.

So Kamua had waited, staring out of his window. He had seen the planes come down and the fires starting. But they were not close enough to worry him. And he was not yet old enough to appreciate what was happening. He didn't like the fact that the lights would not work. He was scared of the dark. Monsters lived in the dark. And by the time the sun was fully set he could see nothing in the stygian darkness of the streets below. It was as if he were floating on a raft above a calm black sea of emptiness. Silent. Blind.

Gramma had kept asking for water but, after one glass, the taps no longer worked. The miracle of running water ceased as the pipes ran dry and the pumps at the water towers functioned no more.

So Gramma had pleaded with him. Imploring him for water as her body tried desperately to flush the sugar out of her system. As the night progressed. Her lack of memantine pills had allowed her dementia full rein and she started to scream and swear at Kamua, flashing her withered genitals at him, licking her lips lasciviously, calling him son of Satan and begging him to defile her.

Finally the little boy had locked her in her room. By morning she had stopped banging on the door.

Kamua decided that he needed some help. Adult help. He knew that his mother always filled Gramma's prescription for her meds at the drugstore on the corner. The man behind the counter always smiled at them and greeted mother like a friend. Kamua would go to him and ask for help.

He took the keys, closed the front door, went to the elevators and pressed the call button. But nothing happened. No lights. Nothing. So, with a child's acceptance, he started down the stairs.

It took him fifteen minutes to reach the ground floor. He left via the front of the building. Immediately he saw that things were not right. Cars were stopped in random positions all over the road. The glass fronts to the shops were all broken or the steel shutters were pulled down and padlocked with massive brass locks. The street was littered with smashed consumer goods. A radio, half out of its retail package, a broken TV, splintered beer bottles, the pavement still damp from the spilt contents. Kamua didn't know what looting was. He had never been taught the concept. All that he could see was that the dark had made bad things happen.

The drug store was shut. The steel doors had been pulled down and locked. There were bright shiny scars on the doors where people had tried to smash their way in. But the doors had held.

Kamua stood in front of the store for a while. Some people walked by. Mainly teenagers. Some single adults. No one even looked at the little boy. They did not know him. He was not their responsibility. Eventually Kamua turned and walked back to his apartment block, went in the front and started the laborious climb back up.

On the twelfth floor he came across a fat man lying on the stairs. His hands were curled in front of his chest and his face was bright red. He was making strange grunting noises. Kamu a was scared but his politeness won out and he greeted the man.

But the fat man just stared at the little boy and grunted, his breath rasping in and out like he was drowning. Kamua stood with him for a while and then continued his upward travel.

He unlocked his front door, closed it behind him and went and sat on the sofa. He stared at the TV. Blank. Lifeless.

He would wait for his mommy.

And then everything would be all right.

***

There were three of them. Two of them had spent the bulk of their adult lives fighting their way up the corporate ladder until they had achieved the level of success that was measured by the position and square footage of your office. The higher up, the more senior. The bigger the footage the more valuable. Both of them, Mary Blithe and Conran Fisher, had offices on the same floor. The 63rd floor of the London Shard. However, Conran's office measured out at six square foot more than Mary's. Hence, he was senior. Just.

The third person was Winston Dube. He was the cleaner for the observation deck of the Shard situated on the 72nd floor and measuring around 8000 square feet or roughly ten times the size of Conran's office.

So, according to the logic used by Conran and Mary – Winston was the most senior of the three. By quite a long stretch.

However, none of this mattered. All that mattered to the three of them was the fact that they had been trapped in the elevator around the 50th floor. It was pitch black. They had been there all night.

And they were now starting, quite understandably, to panic.

'I need to pee,' said Mary. Her voice less of a statement and more a whimper.

'Hold it,' retorted Conran. 'Help will be here soon.'

'What makes you think that?' Asked Winston. 'I mean, we've been here all night. I'm not sure what the time is but I guess that it's late morning. Something's wrong, man. Something is seriously wrong.'

'Well what do you suggest?'

'Nothing to suggest, dude. All that we can do is wait.'

'Exactly.'

'Yeah,' answered Winston. 'Exactly.'

The smell of urine enveloped them. Acrid and pungent. Like distilled fear.

'Sorry,' whispered Mary.

She started to cry.
And they waited.

***

HM Belmarsh prison, or Hellmarsh as the inmates call it, is a category A prison situated in the South East of London.

The prison service manual states that Category A prisoners are: "Those whose escape would be highly dangerous to the public or national security. Offences that may result in consideration for Category A or Restricted Status include: Attempted murder, Manslaughter, Wounding with intent, Rape, Indecent assault, Robbery or conspiracy to rob (with firearms), Firearms offences, Importing or supplying Class A controlled drugs, Possessing or supplying explosives, Offences connected with terrorism and Offences under the Official Secrets Act."

In other words, Belmarsh prison is filled with some very bad people.

But there is nothing to worry about. Belmarsh is a state of the art facility. High walls, well trained guards and a system of electronically controlled Mag-locks that secure every door on every cell. Even in the event of an EMP or similar power outage there is a hardened back up battery that keeps the cells secure. The batteries last for sixteen hours.

Or until 10.00 am in the morning.

It is now 10.01 am.

Belmarsh houses approximately 880 inmates.

Or, to put it more correctly - Belmarsh used to hold 880 inmates.

Chapter 4

Hogan had managed to snatch a couple of hours of intermittent sleep but he was still feeling strong. Unusually so. His vision crystal clear, his body humming with energy. Alert. Ready.

The water was no longer running so the indoor plumbing could no longer be used. The Marines had erected three chemical toilets behind the embassy. They had also taken stock of all of the bottled water, sodas and food, worked out the necessary requirements for everyone and concluded that they had enough food for seven days. Ten if they severely restricted rations. The bottled water would only last another four days.

But water shouldn't be a problem. After all, they were a mere stone throw from the river Thames and a couple of Aquatabs in a drum of river water would purify it to a potable stage.

Liz had asked that one of his Marines go outside the embassy and conduct a recce. Hogan had decided to do it himself. And after thinking about it for a while, he had furthermore decided to conduct the recce in full combat gear as opposed to civvies. He wasn't sure exactly what was going on out there and a Marine never wants to be outgunned.

His men rolled back the gate and he slipped out. There was no one on the street. It wasn't a residential area. He walked down Nine Elms road and turned right before the boating lake into Chelsea Bridge road. He crossed the bridge over the Thames and walked into Chelsea.

There were groups of people walking along the embankment next to the river. Some groups as small as two or three. Other groups, or gangs more likely, as large as thirty, maybe forty people strong. Some people glanced at him but the combat gear and SAW light machine gun caused their eyes to keep moving so as to avoid confrontation.

As he continued he passed the Lister private hospital. A man in a white coat stood on the steps, smoking. Deep bruises of fatigue under his eyes. Face pale. Unshaven.

'Hey,' he called out. 'Soldier.'

Hogan walked towards him. 'Sir.'

'Where are the rest of you?' The doctor asked.

'There is no rest of us, sir,' replied Hogan. 'I am an American Marine gunnery sergeant seconded to the embassy. I'm doing a recon.'

'Have you got any idea what's going on?'

Hogan shook his head. 'Huge power outage, sir. Probably an EMP. Are you all right? How are things going in there?' Hogan pointed to the hospital.

The doctor shrugged. 'Not good. Thank Christ that we're so small. Two operating theatres. Lost both patients when the power went and the backup generators didn't kick in. But we don't have anyone on life support so small mercies.' He took a pack out and offered.

Hogan shook his head. 'Gotta go, sir. But if I were you, I'd batten down the hatches. Lock the doors and windows. Things are going to get ugly soon and any place with drugs is going to be fair game for the criminal elements.'

The doctor nodded his understanding.

Hogan turned and carried on walking. Not looking back.

As he approached Sloane Square he started to see more people on the streets, mostly walking aimlessly. Like car crash survivors or seriously hung over party goers. Most of the shop windows were broken and the convenience stores had been totally emptied as people stripped them for drinks and food. Drugstores had been similarly denuded, the thin veneer of middle class civilization peeling back in less than forty-eight hours to reveal the savage survivor lurking beneath.

He saw the first dead body lying on the road outside the Sloane Club. Older man, business suit, glasses. Hands clutched to his chest in the classic heart attack position. A mere twenty yards on, another body. This time a teenage male. Body twisted and broken. Obviously the victim of a severe beating. Blood lay pooled around his head. Dark. Already drying to a crust.

Hogan took a right turn and double-timed it through Belgravia. He paused every now and then to get his bearings, amazed at how few people were on the street in an area that was normally shoulder-to-shoulder. He assumed that they were hiding in their apartments, waiting to be told what to do. He ran into Eaton Place and turned right, heading towards the Belgravia police station in Buckingham Palace road.

He went past the Budget rent-a-car and noted that the windows had been smashed in, the offices trashed. He wondered dimly what anyone had expected to find there worth looting. Rental agreements? Car freshener?

The police station loomed up on his left and he jogged around to the front.

Two young constables stood in front of the building, standing at the bottom of the steps. They were both carrying the new upgrade of the L85. As Hogan appeared around the corner they both whipped their rifles up and drew a bead on him.

'Halt!' Shouted the one. 'Put your hands above your head.'

Hogan stopped in front of them. He didn't raise his hands.

'Hands up,' screeched the youngster.

'Settle, son,' said Hogan. 'No need to overreact. My name is Nathaniel Hogan, Marine Master Gunnery Sergeant American Embassy.'

'Get down on your knees,' continued the constable.

Hogan shook his head, 'Do me a favor, son. Fetch your inspector. I'd like a quick chat.'

'Knees!'

'In your dreams, boy,' replied Hogan. 'Marines kneel for no one.' He swiveled his M249 to bear on the two constables. 'Your inspector. Now, constable, before I lose my sense of humor and decide to play rat-a-tat on your ass.'

The constable who had not yet spoken turned on his heel and sprinted into the building.

Hogan stood facing the remaining constable. Relaxed. Weapon brought to bear. A slight sardonic smile on his face.

Within a minute the other constable returned followed closely by a man in an inspector's uniform. He was much older than the young guards. His hair cropped short, gray at the temples. A moustache, small gold rimmed round spectacles. He carried a Heckler & Koch MP5.

He nodded at Hogan. 'Master Gunnery Sergeant.'

'Inspector,' replied Hogan.

'How can we help?'

'I'm attached to the American Embassy, inspector. Simply doing a recce and thought that I should run by and see if you have any idea what's happening.'

The inspector took his spectacles off and rubbed the lenses on his shirtsleeve. 'No idea, sergeant. Our chaps think that it may be a nuclear strike of some sort. No communication, no power. Frankly, we're in the dark, both literally and figuratively.' He replaced his specs. 'What about you chaps?'

'Same as, inspector. But one thing I know for sure, it's going to get worse. Much worse. Well, I better be going. Got an embassy to take care of.'

'Hold on, old chap,' said the inspector. 'Afraid that we can't have you running around

London with a machine gun. We may be in the throes of some sort of disaster but that type of thing is illegal, don't you know? Hand your weapons over and you can continue.' The inspector pointed his sub machine gun at the Marine and the two constables followed suit.

Hogan simply smiled and shook his head. 'I'm going back to the embassy. Don't be an asshole, inspector. The time for certain laws has come and gone. And any law that says you gotta try to take the weapon off a Marine has long since passed its sell-by date.'

The sergeant walked backwards, slowly and then turned and jogged off. Back towards the embassy, heading down Pimlico road. About half way down the road he ran into a group of about thirty teenagers. All male, around fourteen to sixteen. Most of them were pushing supermarket trolleys piled high with looted electronic equipment. Laptops, tablets, televisions and projectors. State of the art gear reduced to the level of inefficient paperweights by the pulse. A lesson in stupidity.

He slowed to a fast walk and they parted before him like a shoal of baitfish before a shark. One of the braver ones flicked a mocking salute at him. Hogan grinned.

'Been shopping, boys?' He asked.

'Fo shore, military man,' quipped the saluter. 'We's been getting ourselves some end-of-the-world discounts. Figure that when this is all over we's gonna set up shop, make some serious money.'

The Marine raised an eyebrow. Said nothing. What was the point? He gave a small wave and started jogging again. Within ten minutes he was once again crossing the Chelsea Bridge. When he looked down at the Thames he could see many more people than before. Thousands lined the banks with buckets and bottles, seeking water because the pipes were now completely dry. There were around nine million people in London and approximately fifty miles of river frontage. This means that, if everyone went to the river to claim some water there would be ninety-four people per every yard of water frontage. It won't be long, thought Hogan, before fights are going to break out. Serious fights.

He double-timed it back to the embassy and his men let him in.

A group of embassy employees were gathered at the bottom of the steps. Talking in hushed tones as if at a funeral. They were obviously waiting for him.

'Sitrep, Master Guns,' said Liz.

Hogan thought for a few seconds before he spoke. He needed to get his message across without causing a panic.

'Things are on the verge of meltdown, ma'am. Water supplies throughout the city have been depleted. All of the food shops are empty. Looting has taken place on a grand scale. The police seem more intent on protecting themselves than laying down the law and, to be honest, there's not much that they can do. I guess that full-scale riots will start in the next couple of days as water becomes critical and people converge on the river. Days after that people will be fighting over what food is left. And then medication. People will kill for insulin for their children, antibiotics, pain relief. I reckon that people will start trying to get into the embassy over the next couple of days. Especially if they see that we are inside and alive, they will assume that we have supplies of food, water and drugs. We do, but as you know, not much. The London embassy was never designed for a siege. If we were in Iraq or such, things would be different. But we aren't. And that's about it, ma'am.'

'So what do you advise, Master Gunney?'

'We move out, ma'am. There's twenty-seven of us including my boys. We need to get into the country or to the coast. The city is going to become a living hell over the next few days. My Marines can protect everyone but we won't be able to provide food. There simply isn't any left. Out in the countryside we have a better chance. Not much, but better.'

The Deputy Chief of Mission shook her head. Sighed. 'Really, Master Guns. I must say, you are a disappointment. Firstly, they are not your Marines. They are the United States' Marines. And, secondly, your only advice is to run away? We are Americans, sergeant. We do not run away from problems, we stay and we fix them. Now, this is what I want; put together a plan on how we can sort this out. Put together a foraging team and send them out to find food. Buy it if necessary. Start stockpiling water from whatever source we can. I am sure that our government will be sending help soon. This is an interim problem, sergeant, not the end of the world.' She smirked at him, her face a mask of scorn. 'Carry on, master gunnery sergeant.'

'No, ma'am,' said Hogan. 'I don't think so. If anything I have understated the situation. We have over eight million people in less than six hundred square miles. The roads will be packed with people streaming from the city. Think Moscow, Second World War. No sanitation, armed gangs, Looney tunes with no more access to their Valium. Total chaos. The sooner we all leave the easier it will be.'

'Mountains out of molehills, Master Guns. Now, are you going to do as I say?'

Ordinarily Hogan would have merely agreed. Regardless of what he thought. The Deputy Chief of Mission technically outranked him and Marines followed orders. Marines always followed orders.

But I was as if someone had infiltrated his consciousness and planted an overwhelming desire to rebel. Filled him with a desperate need to leave. An overpowering yearning to pack up and head North. He shook his head but it was no use, he simply could not fight the compunction that was overriding his training.

'With all due respect, ma'am. You are out of your bloody mind. We need to put this to the vote. I know that, technically, you outrank me, but things have changed. Ma'am, things are all messed up. We are drowning in crap and all that you can do is complain about the smell.' Hogan raised his voice. 'Listen up, people. As you know, I have just completed a recce of the surrounds and I can tell you that this city is fast turning to crud in a basket. I recommend that we skedaddle out of here ASAP, head for the countryside. It's gonna be tough but to stay here is to die. I will be leaving in half an hour. Those who wish to come are welcome. Those who want to stay, may God protect you.'

The Marine master gunnery sergeant pushed his way through the crowd and into the embassy. Two of his men met him inside, Manson and Sculley. He gave them a quick rundown of the situation. Neither reacted in the way that he thought they would. They avoided eye contact. Uncomfortable.

'Speak, Manson. What's the problem?'

'No problem, Master Guns. It's just that, well, don't you think that command will send someone to sort everything out? I mean, the fleet or something? If we watch our rations we could have enough for a couple of weeks and by then the brass will have sent backup.'

Hogan shook his head. 'Manson, I don't want to sound like some sort of disaster-monger, but what if there is no fleet? What if this EMP has affected everyone? Then there's no help. Not now, not ever. And by the time that you realize it things will be too late. You'll all be screwed. Trust me, I'm not sure how I know but I just do, we gotta get out of the city and head North.'

But Hogan could see that he'd lost them. The enormity of the situation, added to the fact that Marines did as they were told and never ran, had caused a general shutdown. A lifetime of relying on "them" to take control meant that their perceived best course of action was to wait for "them" to bring help. Hogan didn't say anything else. There was nothing else to say. And in pint of fact he wasn't even sure himself why he was feeling such an overwhelming desire to leave.

The master gunnery sergeant went to the small armory, grabbed a USMC equipment pack. He loaded it with an entrenching tool, sunglasses, a selection of canteens, two Strider SMF knives, extra water purification tablets, matches, two more first aid kits, two extra mags for his 45, three belts of ammo for his main weapon and another one hundred rounds for the Colt. Finally a pack of five First-Strike meals and a handful of the new Soldier Fuel energy bars and a carton of cigarettes.

He strapped the pack on and left the building.

No one spoke as he walked out. The two Marines on the gate nodded their goodbyes as they allowed him through.

He did not look back so he did not see the smirk on Liz Tutor's face as she shook her head in displeasure. Confident in her decision to stay

Confident in the power of the United States of America. And confident that soon the world would return to being the civilized, electrically powered marvel that it should be.

Marine master gunnery sergeant Nathaniel Hogan turned the corner and disappeared from sight.

Overhead the sky still glistened with multicolor lights in an unprecedented orgy of gamma radiation.

Chapter 5

The first day of Hogan's journey had been the worst. Unlike before, London was now choked with people as they realized that to stay in the city was to die. There were people looting, people searching for water and drugs, people simply milling around in groups, their faces blank with dull incomprehension.

Fights and gunshots were a constant thing and one couldn't travel more than a city block without coming across some form of violence.

There were also large swathes of the city that were on fire, primarily due to the huge number of airplanes that had come crashing down and the inability of any firefighters to do anything about it.

But people avoided confrontation with the Marine. The SAW, the Colt 45, the webbing and body armor, all wrapped around a six foot four, two forty pound plus delivery vehicle, added up to something worth avoiding. There were easier targets. More vulnerable targets. And in this case, that more vulnerable group pretty much included anyone else in the greater London area.

Hogan only got involved in two scuffles. The first one involved a middle-aged woman, a shopping trolley and three young men. It was your basic hi-jack. They wanted her trolley full of goods and she didn't want to give it to them. Hogan had decided the issue by smacking the three men in the head with the butt of his SAW and knocking them unconscious. The middle-aged woman had then told him off for being both American and violent. The Marine contemplated slapping the stupid woman in the face but instead he simply shrugged and walked off.

The second event was far more harrowing. A group of teenagers had gathered around an old man and his ancient dog, a black Labrador, and they were stoning the dog to death. Its limp form already lay under a pile of rocks and half bricks. The old man was trying to cover the hound with his own body but the teenagers would kick him aside and then continue their stoning.

Hogan stepped in front of the dog and held his hand up.

'Stop,' he yelled. 'What's going on?'

'Piss off, soldier,' yelled the one boy as he threw a rock at the Marine.

Hogan took a step forward and whipped out a straight-arm punch into the hoodlums face. His nose broke with a crunch and his two front teeth snapped off at the roots. He went down like a rag doll.

The rest of the group pulled back.

'Hey,' shouted a girl. 'That's not right, you bastard. The dog bit me. It should be put down.'

'Oh yeah?' Asked Hogan. 'Where'd it bite you?'

She held up her hand. There was a vaguely discernable red mark on the back of it. A scratch. Maybe a bump. Probably nothing.

In the background he could hear the old man crying as he stroked his dying dog.

It took all of the Marine's willpower to stop opening up on the group of teenagers.

'Get out of here,' he said. His voice little above a harsh whisper. 'Go now, before I kill you.'

The teenagers fell over each other in their haste to escape the gaze of the massive armed warrior in front of them. As soon as they were at a safe distance they turned and shouted a few cuss words. Then they disappeared.

Hogan knelt down next to the old man. 'Are you all right?'

The man looked up at the Marine with red-rimmed eyes. 'They killed Monty,' he said. His voice barely a croak. 'He licked the girls hand and so they killed him. They said he was a smelly old dog and they threw stones at him.'

Hogan put his hand on the dog's neck to feel for a pulse but his master was correct. Monty had drawn his last breath.

'I'm sorry,' said Hogan. But the old man did not respond. He simply sat next to his dead companion. Tears rolled slowly down his face, zigzagging through the wrinkles and lines on his skin.

The Marine stood up and walked away. When he reached the corner and glanced back, the old man was still stroking the dog.

And weeping.

That night the Marine slept in a hedgerow behind a house. Hidden and out of the way.

Chapter 6

The next day he found himself walking through an area where the houses were further and further apart. The fences and gates got larger and higher with more gold paint. Some had hi-tech guardhouses attached to them.

He stopped outside one house that sported a particularly garish set of gates complete with a massive golden coat of arms. For some reason the gates looked familiar and then Hogan remembered why. He had seen these gates on the television some three or four weeks before. They belonged to an American movie star and producer who had married an English girl and moved to the United Kingdom.

He had been interviewed in front of his mansion where he gave a speech, full of his trademark humble Southern expressions and down-home attitudes. He told of how he loved the unique smallness of the country, the essential 'realness' of the people. Then he had proceeded to purchase a house in the never-never land of footballers, PRO gurus and media moguls. Parents who gave their children monikers like Reignbeau or Jermajesty or Moonunit. People who had sold their souls to the devil to garner their ten minutes of fame. People who had no idea that, in the post pulse dark age that had now come upon them, they had traded all to the father of lies merely to become someone who used to be somebody before the world had gone to crap.

Now it was their time to learn that the devil truly is in the small print.

Hogan started to walk again, when he heard someone calling him.

'Hey, buddy.'

He turned to see a large, crew cut man in a tight black suit standing the other side of the gate.

'Can I help you?' Asked the Marine.

The crew cut man smiled. 'Semper Fi, master gunnery sergeant. Private first class, Thomas Kowalski, retired from the corp and living the dream, sir.'

Hogan smiled. 'Oorah, pfc. Once a Marine always a Marine. What can I do you for?'

'Could you come inside, Master Guns?' Asked Kowalski. 'We spotted you coming down the road and my boss would like to have a chat with you.'

Hogan shrugged. 'Why not, pfc. Lead the way.'

The pfc. took out a bunch of keys,

unlocked the gate and opened it just enough for Hogan to squeeze through, closing it behind him.

They walked up the long sweeping driveway towards the house. The drive was covered in white marble chips and bordered by oak trees. Old fashioned lamps and water features also abound but neither worked. The fountains were not natural and the gas lamps were electrical replicas.

'What puts you in these parts of the woods, master gunnery sergeant?' Asked Kowalski.

Hogan gave the pfc a quick rundown that was full of Marine acronyms like ASAP and CQC and OFP.

Kowalski's story was simpler. He had resigned from the corps after Gulf War One, gone into private security and ended up as bodyguard and head of security for mister Hollywood.

They arrived at the entrance to the house. Hogan could see the tail rotor of a helicopter to the right of the sprawling mansion. In the near distance were horses. Peacocks roamed the gardens braying loudly, like donkeys.

The two Marines mounted the sweeping marble steps to the massive front door. Kowalski let them in. The master of the house was standing in the entrance hall and he walked straight up to Hogan, his hand out, multi-million dollar smile lighting up his face. It was a strange feeling for the master gunnery sergeant. He had seen the man's image so many times it felt as if he knew him. The man shook his hand warmly and then put his arm around him, leading him from the entrance through to a sitting room.

'Welcome,' he said to Hogan. 'We saw you coming down the road and I told Kowalski to extend my invitation to you. Us Americans must stick together.'

'Thanks,' said Hogan. 'How did you know that I was American?'

'Kowalski knew. The uniform. The weapons.' He went to a sideboard and gestured to an array of bottles. 'A drink? No ice I'm afraid but I have twenty year old scotch, Russian vodka, French cognac.' He poured himself a whisky. And walked to the window.

Hogan shook his head. The man was starting to irritate him a little. He talked without pause, never waiting for an answer or even expecting one.

'Right, gunny…'

Kowalski visibly flinched.

'Sorry, sir,' interjected Hogan. 'Were you ever in the Marine Corps?'

'No. But I did play a Marine once. Sergeant Major Tellman. DSC. Got an Oscar for that one. Best supporting. Man I was good.'

'Regardless, sir,' continued Hogan. 'You were never an actual Marine, only a pretend one. And pretend Marines don't get to call me gunny. No way. You, sir, may call me Hogan or Nathaniel or Master Gunnery Sergeant or even Marine. Just not, gunny. Ever.'

The actor nodded, unaffected. 'Fair enough, Nathaniel. Now, I'm not sure why you're in the area but I do know one thing. This is your lucky day. Nathaniel, none of us are sure what has happened out there,' he swept his hand across the landscape as he talked. 'We may never know. But one thing…'

'Sir,' interjected Hogan. 'We have a pretty good idea what has happened. There has been some sort of electromagnetic pulse, either man made or natural, we aren't one hundred percent sure, but it has knocked out all of our electronic and electrical capabilities. Over the last few days complete anarchy has taken over. People are dying in their hundreds of thousands and I see no immediate end to this. To all intents and purpose we have been reduced to the dark ages and things will get worse.'

'Well, rather a bleak outlook, Nathaniel,' said mister Hollywood. 'Nevertheless it brings me to my point. I would like you to stay here, with my family, until things get sorted out. I believe that the more Americans and the more weaponry that we have here the safer we will be. We have enough food to last a substantial time. Maybe as long as ten days. By then the government, US or other, will have sorted this mess and I can promise you, you will be substantially rewarded. Not only in monetary terms but also socially. You will become part of my inner circle. Hollywood premiers. A certain degree of fame. Maybe even get the odd role in the movies. All the good things, Nathaniel. So, can I show you your room?' He smiled at Hogan once again. A full one thousand megawatt Hollywood blinder.

Hogan shook his head, more to himself than anyone in the room.

He held his hand out to Kowalski. 'It's been a pleasure, Marine.'

Kowalski shook it. 'Oorah, Master Guns.'

Hogan turned to Hollywood. 'Sir, for once in your life listen up and listen good. It's all over. Your ten days food, you better ration it to last at least a month. Now, use Kowalski here, the American taxpayer has paid almost one million dollars to train him to this point, so utilize his expertise. Send out some recons in force, fact-finding and food acquirement. Set up watches. Be aware. But, this is the most important thing; you have to accept that there will be no miraculous governmental intervention. No cavalry, no column of hummers with MRE's and Coke and gum to chew. This is it, Hollywood man. Lights out, curtain down. It's reality time.'

There was a long pause while the actor stared at Hogan. And then he clapped. 'Brilliant. Man that was intense. "It's reality time". Man,' he continued. 'You have got it. You know, Nathaniel, you could play yourself when they do the movie about this. Perfect man, perfect.'

Hogan snorted in disgust, turned on his heel and walked to the entrance. Behind him he could hear the actor running through his speech. 'It's reality time. Lights out, curtain down…it's goddamn reality time.'

Kowalski walked with Hogan.

'Look, master gunnery sergeant,' he said. 'Sorry about that. These actor dudes don't deal well with reality.'

Hogan shook his head. 'What the hell? Is he simple or something?'

'Nah,' said Kowalski. 'He's famous. Comes down to the same thing. Guy earned millions and got world recognition for doing sod all, where's you and I spent the last ten years of our lives getting shot at for minimum wage. Still, he hired me and where he goes, I go.'

'Semper Fidelis,' said Hogan, repeating the Marine Corp logo in Latin. 'Always Loyal,' he translated.

'To a fault, Master Guns,' said Kowalski. 'To a goddam fault.'

He unlocked the gate and Hogan walked through. He didn't look back and Kowalski said no more.

Chapter 7

Ayoka Falana was born in the small rural village of Nakanda some thirty-five miles outside of Lagos in Nigeria. They had no running water save a hand operated pump in the middle of the village, courtesy of UNICEF and their "Water for Africa" project. Their only electricity was an old petrol driven Yamaha generator given to the village by the "Help Africa Foundation". After it had run out of gas there was no money to get any more, so it simply stood outside the headman's hut and rotted away.

But now Ayoka was in one of the most sophisticated cities in the world. London. And more specifically, in the Royal Chelsea Hospital in Chelsea, London. And the major difference between London and her home village, was that in the hospital in London there was no hand pump for water. So she, and hundreds of others around her, were slowly dying of dehydration.

The irony of the situation did not strike Ayoka. She was not a person who had ever thought in terms of irony or sarcasm or paradox. She thought in more simple terms, she worked hard and she usually got what she wanted.

Although she had never formally attended school her mother had taught her to read and write to a rudimentary level and, from the age of fourteen, she had helped out in the district's local clinic. Rolling bandages, sterilizing instruments and cleaning up. By the age of fifteen she had decided that she wanted to be a nurse. A real one with a nice white uniform and a hat and sensible shoes and a watch that hung from a chain on your breast.

Both her mother and father had approved of her ambition so, the two of them had saved every spare cent that they earned. By the time Ayoka was nineteen years old, they had saved enough to bribe one of the corrupt officials at the Babalola State University to issue her with a fake nurse's degree.

Her proudest moment of her life was when her father returned home from the university and presented her with the certificate.

Ayoka Felana BSc (Hons) Nursing.

She had immediately applied for a nursing post in London, England and had been accepted by all three hospitals that she had applied to.

The entire extended family had banded together to buy her airplane ticket and she had been promised a room in Earls Court with a distant relative for the first month.

She had arrived in London on a Saturday morning; spent the rest of the weekend acclimatizing and started work on the Monday.

That was the day of the first pulse.

It was now 72 hours later.

When the pulse had struck and the entire building was plunged into powerless darkness, the first effects were felt in the operating theaters. All of the theaters were internal rooms with no access to natural lighting. All operations are carried out under HD-LED lighting and the air is controlled through a pressurized laminar flow system. So when the power went and the backup generators were unable to kick in, the operating theaters were plunged into utter pitch black. This, combined with the fact that the anesthetic machines could no longer operate meant that patients were waking up in the middle of their operations in the stygian darkness of hell.

Open heart surgery, stomach surgery, lung surgery. Patients screaming in agony, thrashing around, falling off the operating tables while surgeons and nurses stumbled around in the dark, stepping on the patient's exposed insides. Crushing and maiming. Scalpels cutting into fumbling hands and contaminated needles puncturing groping fingers.

In the neonatal ward thirty-two babies in incubators died within eight minutes.

All patients on life support died within minutes.

By that evening over ninety percent of the patients in the intensive care unit had died.

The next day was far worse. The nine elevators were inaccessible and seven of them had patients prepped for surgery. By that stage, seven out of the nine lifts contained at least one dead body. Water also ran out that morning.

And then the fires started. Doctors were attempting to provide primary care via candle and firelight and it was only a matter of time before a bottle of surgical spirits came into contact with a naked flame. The resulting explosion burned to death two doctors and a mother in labor. The child survived until the next day when it succumbed to burns and infection. The fire was contained via the use of fire extinguishers, one of the few things that still worked.

By that evening the dead and dying lay everywhere. The toilets didn't work and the corridors ran with raw sewage. The stench of death and decay filled the stagnant building like a miasma. Rioting and full scale looting started at around six that evening as people, desperate for diabetic insulin, antibiotics and pain relief stormed the hospital and ransacked it in a frantic search.

The looters started more fires that spread quickly.

And, almost 72 hours to the minute after the pulse, Ayoka Falana, dehydrated and exhausted after three days without sleep, succumbed to smoke inhalation.

Her last thoughts were that her family, with their lack of modern amenities, would most probably never even know that the pulse had ever occurred.

Chapter 8

Hogan had continued walking for five days. He was heading due north, figuring that the areas that would be the least affected by the pulse would be the most rural ones. And he reckoned that the Highlands of Scotland were about as rural as it ever got.

But in the back of his mind he felt that there was another reason he kept going that way. An overriding pressure that nagged at him constantly, drawing him northwards like iron to a loadstone. The same compulsion that had caused him to quit his post. He shook the feeling off and continued simply putting one foot in front of the other. Humping north.

Sticking to the side roads, paths and fields as much as possible he made about twenty miles a day. He slept rough, always in the open as opposed to in a building. Under bushes, hedges, copses of trees. Buildings would either already contain people or they would attract people. And now the word, 'people', could just as easily read, 'predator'. Hogan wasn't afraid of anyone but there is little that one can do if someone smacks you in the head with a shovel while you are asleep. So at night he went under cover and hid.

And all the while the sky above him churned in silent colorful beauty as the gamma rays from the massive solar activity painted the heavens with its Auroral display.

The first couple of days had been the worst. The initial trek out of London. Roads packed with people leaving. Shambling along, shoulder to shoulder. Some pushing shopping trolleys, piled high with worthless goods. Paintings, books, ball gowns. He had even seen one person pushing a wheelbarrow with a grandfather clock in it. Hogan knew, within days, that same person would give everything that he owned for a simple plastic bucket to carry water in. Fools.

After the first few miles he started to notice the dead bodies. Every hundred yards or so. Next to the road. Sometimes alone. Sometimes surrounded by family members. Or friends. Heart attacks, strokes, exhaustion. Old and young dying together as the rigors of the new world took their toll on the sedentary lifestyle of the modern man.

A body left out in the open begins to mortify in two to three hours. After twelve hours the smell, a mixture of decayed cheese and rotten eggs, can be detected at five hundred yards. The fact that there seemed to be a dead body every hundred yards or so meant that there was no way of escaping the putrid smell of death if you continued to stick to the roads. And for most, they had little choice but to do so.

As well as the odor of rotting flesh there was also the gut-churning stench of the body-wastes of the hundreds of thousands of people. Some would veer twenty yards or so off the road to defecate, others, exhausted already, would simply evacuate where they stood. The verges on the sides of the motorways were already running slick with tons of human waste.

A country sized petri dish of disease cultures waiting to mature into typhoid, cholera and salmonellosis.

So Hogan pulled off the main roads and struck out across the countryside instead. Even in the countryside he came across bands of wandering people. Families, groups of strangers. Gangs.

All took one look at the Marine and gave him a wide birth.

He left greater London, crossed Herefordshire and into Bedfordshire. Although he had been living in England for over six months before the pulse, Hogan had not traveled outside of London and he marveled at the countryside as he walked. It was a land built in miniature. Small fields, hedges and low stonewalls. Cottages with ceilings a foot lower than the Marines six foot four. Roads so narrow that they wouldn't even constitute a footpath in America.

It was a land of history and quiet dignity. A land that seemed more suited to its current devolution back to the dark ages than it was with the crass modernity that had swamped it a mere week before.

Near the end of the sixth day he breeched a small hill and found himself looking at a twenty-foot high stonewall. In front of the wall was a dry moat, perhaps six feet deep. The wall curved away from him on both sides.

He turned left. At various points along the wall there were arrow slits and a few low towers. The wall was obviously ancient but, just as obviously, was still in very good condition. An impenetrable fortress.

He continued moving, looking for an entrance.

He heard it before he saw it. A crowd of people. A low level hum of talking with the odd shout thrown in. He walked around the curve and saw around sixty people standing in front of a massive set of wooden gates. The gates were closed.

The crowd carried a mixture of weapons, cricket bats, metal pokers, garden forks. A couple of double-barreled shotguns. One even carried a six-foot long pike, its metal head dull with rust.

A man stood on the allure, behind the battlement, above the gate. He wore the full-length black academic gown of a Professor, complete with red hood. In his right hand he held a .22 target rifle. He was not pointing it at anyone.

'I am sorry, people, but I cannot let you in. The students here are my responsibility and I could not ensure their safety if I let a crowd of strangers in. I am very sorry.'

'What about me, Professor?' Shouted a man at the front, his arms raised beseechingly. 'You know me; I'm not a stranger. I run the local post office. Ronnie. Ronnie Bagstone.'

The master shook his head. 'Sorry, Ronnie. No outsiders. Now please disperse. It will do you no good standing out there, my mind is made up.'

'Up yours,' shouted a longhaired man in blue overalls. 'You've got food and water. Let us in or we'll burn the gates down.'

A few others in the crowd shouted their agreement.

Then someone started a chant. 'Burn. Burn. Burn.'

It was quickly taken up by the others. 'BURN. BURN. BURN.'

One of the shotgun wielders took a bead on the master and fired. Fortunately he was loaded with birdshot and the tiny pellets rattled harmlessly off the battlements.

There was a whirring sound as a lighted Molotov cocktail, a glass milk bottle filled with gasoline and topped with a burning rag, sailed over the crowd and burst on the wooden gates. The explosion of gas a dull crump. The master threw a bucket of water over the wall and most of the fire went out.

Things had gone far enough and the Marine's inherent hatred of mobs rose up within him.

He filled his lungs and, in his best parade ground voice bellowed out.

'Stop. Desist what you are doing and step away from the gates.'

The crowd turned as one to stare. And the sight of him was enough to silence them.

Six foot four of fully armed, well pissed off, Marine Master Gunnery Sergeant. Body armor, helmet, massive machine gun and Colt 45.

But the crowd hadn't eaten for three days. And the only water that they had found had been brackish and muddy. In short, they were dying. And dying people scare less easy than those who are full of life.

'Stuff you, Yank,' said the longhaired man. 'Go home to Yank land, you tosser.'

Hogan smiled. 'Wish I could, my friend. But, as that's not going to happen, why don't you all make like sheep and flock off.'

Someone at the back of the crowd threw a rock. It whipped overhead and hit Hogan on the helmet. Immediately a barrage of sticks and stones hailed down on the Marine. He dodged most, reaction speed in the uncanny range. But many missiles struck. And they hurt.

Then, without warning, the crowd charged.

The Marine didn't even contemplate bringing his SAW to bear. These were civilians. Starving, desperate for food and water. Instead he used the butt of the machine gun to protect himself. Smashing left and right in a blurred frenzy of movement. Ten, twelve, fifteen, twenty-five people went down under his blows.

And then it felt like someone had hit him in the chest with a sledgehammer. He glanced down to see two tines of a steel garden fork sticking up through his neck and into his jaw. The longhaired man had stabbed him under his left arm and from behind, slipping past the body armor, smashing his top two ribs, shattering his collarbone and severing his subclavian vein.

Hogan had seen people who had been stabbed there before. It was what the Marines called, 'A career ending wound,' in that, when you got one, you died. End of career.

But if years of training alongside some of the hardest men in the world had taught Nathaniel Hogan one thing, it was never say die.

He drew his colt 45 and started firing as fast as he could. The crowd turned and ran. Except for longhaired man who took two rounds to the face.

Hogan fell to his knees.
Black…

Chapter 9

Liz Tutor, the Deputy Chief of Mission United States Embassy, took a deep breath, held it, let it escape. A slow ragged exhalation that broadcast her fear on all channels. Fortunately she was alone.

It was a few days after the pulse and no one had contacted the embassy.

No Black Hawk helicopters had swooped in to take them home. No convoys of Marines, no couriers, no communication. Nothing.

They were low on food and had already run out of water. She had asked two of the Marines to take a trolley from the embassy workshop, load it with a couple of plastic drums, and go down to the Thames to collect some more.

Manson and Ronaldo had kitted up and she watched them, through her office window, as they pulled the trolley out of the gates and set off down the road.

'Damn,' said Ronaldo. 'I feel like I'm back at basic training, humping drums of water for the man.'

'Someone's gotta do it,' countered Manson.

They continued pushing, down the road, around the corner. The road was almost empty. They were far from residential areas and the embassy had so far attracted little attention from the scavenging gangs of post pulse London.

They headed down Queenstown road towards the river and, as they passed the Millennium Arena they found the road blocked. Two cars had been pushed across it and, on each side, a barricade of furniture. Office desks, chairs, refrigerators. Standing on top of the cars and crowded behind them was a group of men numbering around two hundred plus. Most of them were dressed in the bright blue and yellow striped boiler suits that the government had recently introduced to all prisons holding category A offenders.

Some were holding shotguns, others swords, knives and clubs. A few even had sidearms. Mainly 22 target pistols although there was also the odd 38 in evidence.

The Marines slowed down and stopped in front of the barricade. Safety catches off. Rifles held ready.

A large man, his shaven head tattooed with a swastika, pointed at them. 'What you want here, soldier boys?'

'Water,' answered Manson. 'For the people at the embassy. We're not looking for trouble, so just let us through. We'll fill up our drums and be on our way.'

The big man laughed. 'Can't do, soldier boy. You see, we own this part of the river now. You want water, then you pay us, the Belmarsh boys.'

'What point is there in charging for water?' Asked Manson. 'Money ain't worth crap at the moment.'

'Screw money,' retaliated the big man. 'Food. Weapons. Your sweet ass.' He thrust his hips towards the Marines and the men around him burst into gales of laughter. Some whistled and clapped. 'Trade with us, soldier. Trade or piss off cause we's busy.'

'Damn you, crap-for-brains,' shouted Ronaldo as he brought his rifle to shoulder. 'Nobody talks to the Marines like that and gets away with it.'

He shot the big man twice in the chest. The high velocity rounds punched through him and exited out of his back in a spray of red mist. His body slumped slowly to the car roof. His face a mask of surprise.

Normally this sort of reaction would cause a crowd to scatter as they ran for cover. But these were ex-inmates of one of Britain's most infamous prisons. Psychopathically hard men made harder by a system of punishment as opposed to reformation. Men who did not react in the same way as any other normally functioning member of society.

There was perhaps a second of stunned silence and then everyone with a weapon fired back. Shotguns boomed, 22 pistols cracked. Spears and knives and house bricks flew. Even though the Marines were wearing full combat armor, the level of firepower was simply too great. A spear lanced into Ronaldo's throat, smashing his esophagus and slicing his jugular before exiting from the back of his neck. A shotgun blast took him full in the face, blinding him and shredding his flesh from the bone. He was dead before he hit the floor.

Manson slipped his fire selector to full auto.

'Oorah!' He shouted as he pulled the trigger and swung the barrel. The thirty round magazine emptied in under four seconds, the supersonic rounds chewing through at least six people before the rifle clicked empty. The crowd of criminals surged forward like a wave of human violence, swarming around the

Marine, knocking him to the ground, kicking and hitting until his body was merely an inanimate flesh sack full of broken bone.

For a moment the gang of thugs milled around. Purposeless. And then it found its natural level. The hierarchy of the prison system clicked in and the next rung on the ladder stepped up to lead.

Almost a carbon copy of the recently deceased big man except that the new leader's swastika was tattooed on his face.

He jumped onto the roof of one of the cars. 'They killed ours,' he shouted. 'Now we go get theirs. American embassy. Let's go.'

He jumped off the roof and started running. The pack ran after him, ululating, screaming. Laughing. A mobile mass of concentrated vileness acquiescing to the lowest human denominator.

It took them less than fifteen minutes to get to the gates of the embassy and when they did they did not stop. As one they threw themselves at the gates, climbing over one another to gain the top of the steel barricade and jump over.

Years of prison brutality pouring from them like pus from a ruptured boil.

The two Marines at the gate were caught completely by surprise but their training slammed home in seconds and they brought their weapons to bear. They only managed to get off a few shots each before they were cut down.

Someone threw a Molotov at the embassy entrance and it exploded on the front doors, burning fuel spreading into the lobby.

The four remaining Marines who were off duty and asleep, grabbed their weapons and ran for the entrance. Already there were around fifty armed prisoners inside the building. Male members of staff were mercifully executed on sight. Female staff members were punched to the ground and queues immediately formed.

The four Marines sprinted into the entrance lobby, firing from the hip. The Belmarsh boys flipped over desks for cover and fired back. Another Molotov exploded against the wall, spraying the one Marine with burning fuel. He rolled on the floor in an attempt to smother the flames but they were too strong. He jumped up and ran in an aimless circle, screaming in mortal agony.

One of the prisoners found this to be so amusing that he collapsed on the floor in a paroxysm of laughter.

Eventually the burning man fell to his knees and died. Hands curled up in front of his chest. An emolliated sacrifice to the Belmarsh boys.

The Marines were members of one of the paramount fighting forces in the known world. But they were few and the enemy were many. Too many. The Marines took their toll as they killed and killed again. In total they sent eighteen Belmarsh boys to hell before the force of numbers overwhelmed them.

Now the only sound was the crackling of flames and the whimpering and screaming of the women as they were repeatedly raped.

And on the top floor of the embassy, Liz Tutor, the Deputy Chief of Mission United States Embassy, opened the access door to the heliport on the roof of the building and slipped out, closing it behind her. Her face was slick with tears and her body jerked at every scream, every whimper from below.

Why hadn't they come to rescue them?

Where were the troops?

Where were the helicopters?

The fifth fleet?

Sobbing, she undid the lanyard and pulled the Stars and Stripes down from the flagpole. She unclipped it and wrapped it around her like a shawl.

Behind her the door burst open and a gaggle of lunatics scurried in.

'Oho,' one shouted. 'Fresh pussy.'

Liz walked calmly to the edge of the roof and then turned to face the men, the stars and stripes clad her in its glory.

'And this be our motto,' she said. 'In God is our trust.'

She raised a finger at them.

'Damn you all to hell.'

For a short while she flew before her life was crushed from her as she struck the ground.

And the shrieks and whimpers continued.

And the embassy burned.

And old glory slowly turned red with her blood.

Chapter 10

Black…
And then a pinprick of light.
Smell of wood smoke.
Sound of flames.
He blinked.
More light.
He sat up.
Alive!

The room swam into focus. Stone walls. Tall mullioned windows. A fireplace, with fire. And standing at the end of the bed a young woman. Pale skin, deep red hair. Hint of a smile. Before he could say anything she turned and left the room at a fast walk.

On a small table next to the bed he saw a glass of water. He picked it up, two handed, and took a sip. It tasted like fine wine. Heady. Invigorating.

Alive!

The girl walked back into the room followed by an older man. Hogan recognized him. The man who had stood above the gate. The man who had turned the outsiders away.

He pulled up a chair and sat down next to Hogan, the girl stood next to him. 'Greetings, young man,' he said. 'How are you feeling?'

'I'm alive.'

The man chuckled. 'It would appear so.'

'How?'

'Lucky, I suppose.'

Hogan shook his head. 'No one's that lucky. I was dead for sure.'

'Obviously not.'

Hogan started to talk again but the older man flashed him a look and then glanced at the girl. Later, the look said. Not now.

'Can I get you something to eat, sir?' The girl asked.

Hogan nodded. 'That would be much appreciated. How long have I been out?'

'Not long. Only the one night,' answered the man as the girl set off to get Hogan some sustenance. 'After your…altercation with the crowd, they dispersed and we opened the gates and dragged you in.'

'So then, where am I?' Asked the Marine.

'You are a guest at Biggleswich Independent coeducational boarding school, set in the grounds of the fortified Abbey of Lilysworth.'

The girl reappeared with a tray. On it was a bowl of porridge, a glass of milk and small bowl of sugar.

'Just a snack,' said the girl. 'It's almost dinner time, you can have a proper meal then.'

Hogan thanked her and tucked in. It had been years since he had last tasted porridge and it was exactly as he remembered it. Hot, stodgy and sugary. He took a sip of the milk. It tasted odd. Not off, just weird. The older man noticed his expression.

'It's goat's milk,' he said. 'We have a few goats on campus. Apparently it's very good for you.'

Hogan shrugged, downed the rest of it and burped mightily. The girl hid a smile behind her hand.

'Are you up for a walk?' Asked the older man.

Hogan nodded, flung back the bedclothes and swung his legs over the side of the bed. Only then did he notice that he was totally naked except for the bandage around his neck and shoulder. The girl gave a squeak and rushed from the room, her long copper hair streaming behind her like a cape of virtue.

The older man chuckled. 'Your kit is there,' he pointed at a chair in the corner of the room. Hogan's camos were neatly pressed and folded. His helmet, combat armor and weapons lay on the floor next to the chair.

The Marine stood up, walked over and got dressed. He left the armor, battle gear and weapons where they were, except for the pistol that he tucked into his belt.

The older man stood up and held out his hand. 'My name is Jonathan Holt. Most call me, Professor or Prof. I'm easy with all or any.'

Hogan shook the Professor's hand.

'Marine Master Gunnery Sergeant Nathaniel Hogan, American Embassy. Pleased to meet you, Prof.'

Hogan followed the Prof through the tall stone corridors of the school. As they walked the older man gave him the run down.

Although the school was situated in buildings that were in excess of five hundred years old, it was a model of the modern private school or, as the English called it, a public school. The Prof explained that they were the leading charitable school in the country and, as such, had a broad range of students who were chosen from the best and brightest as opposed to the ones with the wealthiest parents.

Unlike the usual English public school, Biggleswich promoted freethinking and a more modern approach to discipline. Scholars were entrusted with their own vegetable allotments on which they grew beans, potatoes and other sundry vegetables. Some ran chickens. The Professor had a small herd of six goats. All produce was harvested by the scholars and handed to the kitchens. The scholars were then paid in privileges, television time, gaming.

Academic achievement also gained privileges as well as accolades such as special items of clothing, different neckties, scarves and badges. In the center of the school was a water well with a non-working electric pump. There was, however, an ancient hand pump that was capable of drawing water up and into a small water tower.

The Prof explained that, as it was school holidays, there were very few scholars at the school. The only ones there were the older students who had stayed on for a few days in order to cram for their forthcoming exams. Now, of course, there was no way that they could leave.

Thirty scholars. Twelve girls and eighteen boys. There were also eight staff that lived on the premises. The Professor, the school nurse, the caretaker and five other teachers.

The Prof also showed Hogan the school armory. Ten 22 target rifles and six air rifles. As well as the weapons, they had a full case of 22LR ammunition. Five thousand five hundred rounds.

They were, to all intents and purposes, a completely self-sustaining community.

'Very impressive, Prof,' said Hogan. 'I'll tell

you something for nothing, though. Those people who tried to get in here are going to come back. If not them then someone else. And next time they won't take no for an answer. You don't know what it's like out there. It's the nine circles of hell.'

'We have a high wall. A dry moat.'

Hogan shook his head. 'Not good enough. Ladders negate walls. Your gate is a weak point. A good volley of Molotovs and you'd be hard pressed.'

'Well then, Master Gunnery Sergeant,' replied the Prof. 'Help us.'

Hogan nodded and they walked for a while in silence. He felt for a pack of cigarettes and was pleased to find them still in his trouser pocket. He took them out, opened, took his Zippo from the half empty pack and offered. The Prof shook his head.

'I'm a pipe man myself,' he said. 'Won't be that for much longer though. Not much baccy here, I'm afraid.'

The Marine lit up. Drew. Exhaled.

'Professor Jonathan Holt,' he said in a thoughtful voice.

'At your service, good man.'

'Why is that name so familiar?'

The Prof shrugged.

Hogan took another greedy hit of nicotine and then stared at the glowing tip of his cigarette for a while. 'Didn't you win the Nobel Prize? Genetics? Biology or something?'

'Guilty as charged,' admitted the Professor. '2016. Nobel Prize for Physiology or Medicine.'

'Didn't you cure cancer?'

The Professor laughed. 'No, Master Guns. We still have no sure-fire cancer killer. I merely helped pave the way to many of the cures that we use today. I discovered that the FoxO gene, present in vast quantities in the common Hydra, was what we now call, the longevity gene. However, people with a surplus of this gene sometimes lived longer but, more often than not it caused their cells to reproduce at a rate that was far too rapid, causing tumors and, ultimately, cancer. I developed a serum that helps to control the FoxO gene. Oddly enough, I wasn't looking to cure cancer; I was looking for the fountain of youth. Still, all's well etcetera.'

Hogan raised an eyebrow. 'Cool.'

'Yes,' agreed the Prof. 'Exceptionally cool. Which brings me to your condition, sergeant. Your, shall we say, miraculous recovery. I have a small laboratory here. Unfortunately much of it has been rendered useless by the current circumstances but I can still do a great amount of research. I wonder if, after dinner, we might spend some time there. I'd like to take a blood sample, some tissue samples and other general readings.'

'Sure thing, Prof,' said Hogan. 'But first some chow. I'm still starving.'

The Professor laughed and then led the way to the dining hall.

Over dinner Hogan fielded many questions about the outside. It was generally agreed by all that the pulse was a natural, or perhaps supernatural, occurrence and the Marine was impressed by the maturity and stoicism shown by the scholars, many of whom were only sixteen years old. Food consisted of potatoes, eggs, green vegetables and a little goat's milk. Bland but filling and nutritionally well balanced.

The girl with the copper hair sat at the next table, chatting to her friends. Hogan couldn't stop himself looking at her. She was tall and self-possessed, her movements confident and economic. Eyes a clear hazel flecked with green. Every now and then she would catch Hogan's glance and smile shyly.

The Prof noticed the Marine's interest.

'That's Maggie,' he said. 'Maggie Turner. Final year scholar. Her parents live in London.

Used to…might still. Lovely lass.'

'Yes,' agreed Hogan. 'Very.'

Hogan and the Prof helped carry the crockery back to the kitchen and then the Marine followed the academic to his laboratory. It was dark now and the Prof illuminated the way with a gas lantern, its small white flame remarkably powerful due to a polished reflector at the back and a large magnifying lens attached to the front.

The laboratory was more of a study than a hospital room. Wood paneled walls, leather chairs, a single stainless steel table with washbowl ran the length of the room, pushed up against the wall. On the one side of it stood a huge standard optical microscope.

'I wonder if you wouldn't mind rolling up your sleeve, right arm, Nathaniel?'

Hogan rolled up his sleeve to expose his arm while the Prof rummaged around in a drawer and came out with a needle and small syringe in aseptic packaging. The Marine held out his arm and the Prof didn't even bother with a tourniquet, as Hogan's median cubital vein stood out on his arm like a steel cable. He drew a full syringe and Hogan pressed his thumb over the site after the needle had withdrawn. Next the Prof asked Hogan to open his mouth and he swabbed the inside of his cheek with a q-tip that he placed into a sterile bag. Finally he opened a single pack, large scalpel blade and took a scraping off Hogan's forearm.

'What now?' The Marine asked.

'Now,' answered the Professor. 'I spend a few hours doing my thing. You, good sir, are free to do whatever you want.'

Hogan spent the next couple of hours wandering around the grounds. It was dark but there was a full moon so he had more than enough light to see by. He noted points where the forest was close to the walls, he noted weaknesses in the construction and he figured on how he would take the place if he needed to.

After that he went to bed and slept well, deep and dreamless.

The next morning he rose early and stood next to his open window, trousers on but still shirtless, while he smoked a cigarette. Behind him someone knocked on the door and then walked in. It was the Professor.

'Good day, Marine.'

'Back at you, Prof. What gives?'

The Professor walked straight up to Hogan and stood close. 'Do you mind if I take a look under your bandage, good fellow? Should be about time to change the dressing anyway.'

'Sure,' acquiesced Hogan.

The Professor unclipped the safety pin that held the dressing tight and nimbly unwound it. As he got below the first few layers the fabric was crusty with dried blood. He finally pulled the last length off with a flourish. A Vegas magician. The big reveal.

'Aha!' He shouted.

Hogan flinched.

'What? What's wrong?'

'Nothing,' said the Professor. 'Everything. Buggered if I know.'

Hogan stared down at the wound in his neck and shoulder. But it was not there. His skin as smooth and unblemished as a supermodel.

'What the hell?' He managed.

'Yes,' agreed the Professor. 'Very what the hell indeed.'

Chapter 11

Sam was six years old. Although, if you asked him he would disagree. He would inform you, quite seriously in his clear firm voice, that he was six and a quarter years old. And he would be correct.

It was pulse plus one week. Sam's father had not come home from work after the pulse. He worked in London in a huge glass building that went up so high that it was on the same level as where God lived. Sam's dad used to say that all decisions made on the top floor went from God, to mister Jenkins to him. The little boy had no idea what his dad actually did but he knew that he was important. Anyone who is removed from God by only one person (mister Jenkins) must be important. Very.

Sam's mom was a stay at home mother. Sometimes dad used to call her a 'Domestic Managerial Engineer', and she would look cross even though Sam thought that it was quite cool being a domestic managerial engineer.

Sam's mom's name was Beverly. Dad used to call her, Lovely.

Lovely had been dead for two days now. Bad men had come to their house and mom had hidden Sam in the secret cupboard under the stairs behind the ironing board. The men made mommy scream and cry for a long time and then they went. The next day Sam had come out of the cupboard. He had tried to give his mommy some water. But it just dribbled all over her face and she didn't move.

The bad men had taken all of the food. But they had left a bag of dog food. The dog food was old. Mom had bought it for Sasha the Labrador but then Sasha had got cancer and went to doggy heaven. No one had thrown away the dog biscuits.

The dog biscuits were very hard but not so bad if you mixed them with water. And Sam had lots of water that he collected from the rain water butt outside the back door.

Sam had put some in his mom's mouth but she didn't eat them. She was beginning to smell bad now. It made Sam feel ill so he took a bowl of dog biscuits and water and crept back under the stairs.

Chapter 12

Commander Ammon rolled up the maps of the kingdom that lay scattered on his campaign table. They were actually unnecessary, used more as a point of focus than actual reference. He knew every square inch of them by heart.

And it didn't matter how many times he looked at them, the outcome was the same. He was winning the battles but, ultimately, he was losing the war. The elves had tried four more mass assaults in the valley and he had repulsed them. For the loss of a mere two hundred warriors he had slain eight thousand of the enemy. Eventually the fallen lay so high and deep as to form a wall of death, preventing any more frontal attacks by the hive. And now, even more than two leagues from the valley, the stench was a palpable thing. An oily taste that coated the back of the throat.

Now, however, the hive had started sending smaller parties, six or seven hundred at a time, over the mountains, seeking out any passable route. Some got through, many did not. But when a group did make its way over the passes the information was immediately known by the rest of the hive and thousands would advance on the same route.

The Commander had formed small mobile groups of fast-reaction Orcs, squads of one hundred including twenty goblin archers. Trolls were too slow to be incorporated. As soon as news arrived of a breach then a century would be dispatched at forced march speed to engage. It was working and, thus far, all encroachments by the hive had been met with total annihilation. But the constant need for preparedness was taking its toll. Not only on the troops but also on the commander himself.

He was not sure how much longer they could continue and, every day, commander Ammon expected another full frontal attack through the valley but this time combined with a few mountain encroachments as well.

If he had been in charge of the hive that is what he would have done,

But then, maybe they were hurting as much as he was.

Maybe.

Seth Hil-Nu, paramount mage, stepped into the commander's tent, pulled up a stool and sat down. He looked exhausted; the skin around his mouth an unwholesome pink instead of the dull gray of health.

'How goes, commander?' The mage asked.

'It goes as the gods will, mage. We win. We lose at the same time. Ultimately…I fear that we are a dying race, the very last of the Fair-Folk. And you, my friend?'

'Tired. However, I have some good news. Perhaps. Well, not really sure, I may be grasping at straws.'

'Straws will do if that is all that we have left to grasp at,' said Ammon. 'Tell your story.'

'I think that I have found a source of Life-Light.'

'You think, or you have?'

'I have. However, I am struggling to track it down. I can feel its pull. It's presence. But it is immeasurably far away, in both space and time.'

'Explain, my friend. Pretend for a moment that I am but a commander of troops and have little knowledge of the arcane workings of the Life-Light and its mysteries.'

'I see,' said Seth wryly. 'You mean, distill four hundred years of bitter study down to a teaspoon of syrup.'

Ammon laughed, the sound a dry cough. Short staccato bursts. 'If possible, my friend. If possible.'

'Well, Ammon, you have used the Life-Light before.'

'Yes, in my own limited way.'

'And how does it feel?'

Ammon thought for a while. 'Powerful. Uneasy. Slightly out of control…'

'Carry on.'

'Discombobulated.'

'A good description, disconcerted. Confused. The reason for that is, the Life-Light itself, although visible to us, is not part of our direct time and place.'

'I don't get it.'

'Let me explain, and please bear in mind that I am attempting to describe an ocean using only a single drop of water. Where does the Life-Light come from?'

'Easy,' said the commander. 'Our sun.'

Seth shook his head. 'We say that, to avoid confusion. However, it comes from a time and place far removed from our sun. By the time it reaches our sun it has already been traveling for some hundred million years plus. When it reaches our sun, which, as we know is simply a massive ball of fire, it affects it in such a way as to distill the Life-Light into an energy that we can use. This is given off in the form of sun flares that manifest themselves visibly as Life-Light. As you know, our mages can convert this Life-Light into the raw energy needed for our magiks. Now, as far as we can deduce, we are dealing with a raw energy that has traveled around ten million trillion leagues and started its trip countless millions of years before we even existed as a culture, we then take this energy, convert through arcane means and release it. To cut to the quick; there is bound to be some fallout. That is what a top mage spends his time controlling – the fallout. Creating magik is easy. Surviving the casting…not so much.'

'Thank you, master mage,' said Ammon. 'Now I am slightly more confused than before. However, if I gloss over my obvious lack of knowledge, you are saying that you think that you have found another source of Life-Light, but you can't pin it down?'

'Yes and no. I will be able to pin it down but, and this is a big but, there is no way that we can use it to effect things here, in this time and place.'

'So, pray my good friend, what is the point?'

'The point, commander, is that I could use it to create a gateway for us to cross over. To go to another time and place where we would be able to use the Life-Light as we did before.'

'You mean – run away. Retreat?'

Seth shook his large gray head. 'No, commander, I mean retire gracefully from a war that we cannot win. It is simply time to move again, as we have done before in our history.'

Ammon said nothing. There was nothing to say. One didn't have to be a genius to work out that, in the long term, the fair folk's position was untenable.

'So, tell me, my friend,' continued Seth. 'How long do we have?'

Ammon took a deep breath. 'It depends on a few factors. If the hive continue in the exact same way, sending forays into the mountains and such, well then…a couple of months. Tops. However, if their queen decides on an all out push, hits us from the mountains and the valley…two, three days. Maybe a week.'

'Worse than I thought,' said Seth.

The two sat in silence for a while. Ammon, thinking. Seth waiting.

Finally, Ammon spoke. 'Find it, Seth. Find our gateway out of here. I will fight as long as I can, but you shall save us. How soon can you do it?'

Seth stood up. 'It will be a tight run race, commander. I will go to my tent now to begin preparations.' The mage bowed formally. 'By your leave, commander.'

Ammon stood and bowed back. 'May success be yours, mage.'

Seth left the campaign tent and Ammon sat back down and prepared to fight a losing war.

Chapter 13

Hogan sat down on the edge of the bed and lit another cigarette, idly noticing that there were only three left in the pack. He hoped that he had another pack in his webbing but wasn't sure.

'It's the FoxO gene,' said the Professor. 'You know, the Hydra longevity gene that I spoke of earlier?'

The Marine nodded. 'I remember.'

'Well,' continued the Prof. 'Your bloodstream is awash with it. Chock-a-block full of longevity genes.'

'But, won't that give me cancer? You said that the FoxO gene grows out of control and creates tumors and cancer and crap. And how have I lasted this long? I should have been dead ages ago.'

The Professor nodded. 'Well, usually. But that's a bit of a broad statement because I've never seen a case like yours before. The only explanation that I can come up with, is that you are a natural carrier of large numbers of the FoxO gene and that, somehow, the Gamma radiation from the pulse has mutated your FoxO genes in some fashion. You see, Nathaniel, it's not simply that your system is flooded with the FoxO gene, the gene itself is mutating. It seems to have attached itself to a virus. This virus is reproducing by taking over the reproductive process of its host cells, you being the host cell. No, the interesting thing is, the virus is living in you in an entirely symbiotic way. In other words, if you die, then it dies. It knows this, so, by using the FoxO gene, it will do its best to prevent you actually dying.'

Hogan thought for a while. 'So, what you're saying is…'

The Professor finished the sentence for him. 'Sergeant, to all intents and purposes, you are immortal!'

Hogan said nothing. What was there to say? There is no social situation or past experience that could have prepared him for such a revelation.

Eventually he settled on. 'Oh.'

The Prof smiled. 'Look, when I say immortal, I could be incorrect. You may very well be susceptible to disease. Also I am not sure how you would respond to massive physical trauma, such as losing your head. You could probably still starve to death and I would assume that oxygen is a necessity. Perhaps, instead of the word immortal we should say, Extremely durable.'

'What, you mean like that bunny in the battery adverts?'

The Prof laughed. 'Actually, sergeant, more than you know. It actually brings me to the second point that I need to make. Do you remember much about the fight that you had before you were stabbed and we brought you in here?'

Hogan nodded. 'Yep. Got attacked by a bunch of desperate people. Didn't want to shoot them so I laid them out instead. Got stabbed. Had to shoot. That's pretty much it.'

'Do you remember how many people you knocked out?'

Hogan shrugged. 'I only had a few seconds. Maybe three. Four?'

'Twenty five,' said the Prof.

'Impossible,' denied Hogan.

'Yet you did it. I saw it with my own eyes. You were supernaturally fast. I could barely keep visual track of you. The fact that you were stabbed at all was simply sheer bad luck. And as well as the speed there was the heat. I could see waves of it pouring off you. Like the heat haze from a jet engine. When we dragged you in you were still hot to the touch.'

'Why?' Asked the Marine.

'Well, it's conjecture again but I figure that the virus has an ability to react to any circumstance that puts the host body, you, in danger. It then uses whatever methods it can to combat this danger to you and, therefore, to itself. In this case, I surmise that it increases adrenalin flow into the body at a geometric rate causing an Adrenergenic storm. This will heighten your senses, speed up both strength and reaction time and dull any sense of pain. Usually this would result in an almost instantaneous event of acute myocardial infarction as your heart literally tears itself apart within a couple of seconds. However, the FoxO virus/gene seems to repair your shattered heart microsecond by microsecond, thus allowing you to function at massively increased rates of strength and speed for relatively prolonged periods of time. This, in turn, gives rise to an exothermic release in the form of heat.'

'So, I'm some sort of Duracell bunny, vampire, human radiator, Hulk-type freak?'

The Professor thought for a while before answering. Finally he said. 'Yes. That about sums it up.'

'Could be worse,' said Hogan. 'I could be trapped in a foreign country with no way of ever getting home due to the fact that a solar flare has smacked us back into the dark ages and the entire world has gone to crap.'

The Marine lit another of his dwindling supply of cigarettes.

'Would you like a little time alone?' Asked the Prof.

Hogan nodded. 'Give me a few minutes so that I can come to terms with the concept of infinity.'

The Prof smiled and left the room.

Nathaniel Hogan simply sat on the edge of the bed and smoked his cigarette. He tried to process what the Professor had just told him but it was impossible. The entire concept simply slid away from him as he tried to pin it down. He wanted to rave. To tell the Prof that he was a bloody idiot. No one could cheat death. No one lived forever…no one survived the injury that Nathaniel had just survived. And especially without even the slightest hint of a scar.

By the time that he had finished his cigarette the Marine had made a decision. He would simply ignore the newfound knowledge. After all, what possible difference would it make to his life in the short term? In the immediate future he was still an exile in a strange country in the new dark ages. The possibility that he may be in this position forever did not fill him with a feeling of happiness. Far from it. But forever is another day and today was here and now.

He stood, finished dressing and went to the dining hall to find some breakfast. There were still a few scholars eating, as was the Prof and the groundsman, mister Conradie, a ruddy faced fat man whom Hogan had met the day before. The breakfast was a pot of the ubiquitous oats porridge, sugar and goats milk. Hogan helped himself to large quantities of it and sat down next to the Professor, greeting him and Conradie as he did so.

'So,' said Conradie. 'The Prof says that you may condescend to give us some advice on beefing up the security around here. Says that you fear the mobs might come back.'

Hogan shook his head. 'No, I said that the mobs will come back. Definitely.'

Conradie smiled derisively. 'Do them no good. High walls. Dry moat. We've got weapons and we're not afraid to use them. No, I think that your fear has got the best of you. And if they do come, I think that you will find that we can handle ourselves pretty well without help from an American. No offense.'

Hogan smiled. 'No offense taken, mister Conradie. Not your fault that you're a self important, know all dick head.'

Conradie spluttered into his milk. 'I beg your pardon?'

'No need to beg, mister, it's just embarrassing,' said Hogan as he lent forward. 'Now listen, Conradie, and listen good. It won't be long. Days, not weeks, and the mob will be back. And there will be more of them, much more. They will be desperate and more organized than the spontaneous rabble that you had here before. Most likely they will end up storming the gates. But first they will attempt to get in over the walls. Particularly the back wall, behind the armory. The stones are loose and there are trees close to the wall. All that they need to do is fell a couple of trees in the right direction and they get a walkway over the wall and into the digs. Once your enemy is inside your perimeter in strength, then you are well and truly screwed and hung out to dry. *Id Est*, Conradie, all dead. Or worse.'

'Sergeant,' Conradie interjected. 'I hardly think…'

'Exactly,' said Hogan. 'You hardly think. Fortunately, I do think. And as soon as I am finished my porridge we will take a walk around the walls and I will tell you what needs to be done and you will see that it is done. Correctly and well and all shipshape. Is that clear, mister Conradie?'

The groundsman stared at Hogan for a full few seconds before he replied. 'Yes, sergeant,' he said. 'I understand.'

'Good. And it's Master Gunnery Sergeant or Mister Hogan. Either or.'

Conradie nodded softly, his head down. Obviously embarrassed. A self-important man brought to bear by a soldier.

Hogan bolted the rest of his porridge down, stood up and gestured with his head to Conradie as he walked to the door. The two of them walked out together. The Prof stayed sitting at the dining table, a look of vague amusement on his face.

After Hogan had left, the Prof turned to a group of scholars that had watched the altercation and he grinned. 'Vociferous lot, our American cousins, aren't they? Still,' he continued. 'Nice to see that ass, Conradie taken down a peg or two.'

There was a general ripple of laughter and the Prof helped himself to more goat's milk.

Hogan strode out towards the back of the monastery walls and Conradie puffed along next to him, his fat wobbling and rolling as he struggled to keep up with the tall, long legged Marine. Eventually Hogan slowed down, knowing that he was simply being childish. But the short fat man seemed to bring out the worst in the Marine.

'I'm sorry if you feel that I misspoke back there,' puffed Conradie.

'You didn't misspeak,' countered Hogan. 'You simply talked crap.'

'Steady, old boy.'

The Marine stopped abruptly, turned and grabbed Conradie by the shoulders. 'Conradie, I'm not trying to usurp whatever position you think that you have here. In fact I'm not even going to be staying here for much longer. However, I am a trained Master Gunnery Sergeant with the US Marine Corps. I have forgotten more about war and defense and protection than you and everyone within a hundred miles will ever know. I have been outside and I can assure you, it is a complete goat orgy! People are killing for a can of soda. So listen up, all I care about are the children. I will tell you how to seal this place up tighter than a duck's ass. I will stay until I deem it safe for me to go and then I shall bugger off and you can continue being the self-righteous turd that you are. Comprendez?'

Conradie nodded.

'Right,' continued Hogan. 'First things first. I want ladders up to the battlements on the back walls. The steps are messed up and I don't trust them. Secondly, get some mortar and seal up the top three rows of stone. They're crumbling. Thirdly, I need to take a group of strong youngsters out today to fell some trees. The forest has grown far too close to the back walls. You'll need the wood for winter at any rate so it's two jobs in one. Also, do you have any twine, lots of it?'

Conradie shook his head. 'I've got a few hundred meters of fishing line. Will that do?'

Hogan nodded. 'Perfect. Even better.'

After Hogan's second admonishment, Conradie had developed a much better attitude and, while not brimming with enthusiasm, did seem to be trying to help.

'Right,' said Hogan. 'You get a team of five boys together with axes, wood saws, perhaps some wheelbarrows. I'm going to tool up and I'll meet them at the gate ASAP.'

Conradie looked puzzled. 'I'm sorry, mister Hogan, but I didn't quite get that. You say, tool-up?'

'Yeah,' agreed Hogan. 'Get ready to rock and roll. You know, weapons hot and ready to go.'

The Marine left the perplexed groundsman and jogged back to his room to get his SAW and body armor. He started putting on the heavy Kevlar jacket and then stopped, smiled, and dropped it on the floor.

'Bugger that,' he said to himself. 'I'm an invincible armor plated long-life mother.'

He slipped on his webbing, lifted the machine gun and headed for the main gates.

Five boys were waiting for him when he got there. Three carrying double handed axes and two had large wood saws and a wheel barrow each.

Conradie introduced them. Hands were shaken and names mumbled. Hogan made a point of asking for the names to be repeated if he didn't get them the first time. A leader always knows his men.

Then the groundsman opened the gate, let them out and closed it behind him.

The group walked slowly next to the walls heading for the back. Hogan took point and discouraged any talking with a look. He could see that the boys were nervous. More so of him than of any alleged nefarious interlopers that may or may not be on the prowl.

When they reached the correct spot, Hogan started them felling the trees closest to the wall. Chopping the trunks opposite to the wall so that they fell safely away from the structure. Two axe wielders would attack one tree, swing at it in rhythm until, after twenty or so swings each, the tree would topple to the ground.

When a tree had fallen he instructed the saw holders to start sawing the logs into two-foot lengths.

The boys were young, strong and fit. But they were soft. City soft. And chopping wood is an extremely rough task. After two hours Hogan called a halt.

'Well done, guys,' he said. 'I'll get Conradie to send another team out to carry all of the wood back. If you could load up the two wheelbarrows then we'll call it a day.'

'Hell, sir,' said the one boy. 'What a pity, so soon and you didn't even get to have a go.'

The rest laughed. Good-natured teasing. Hogan smiled with them, glad that their nervousness has dropped to the point that they could joke around a little.

He put the SAW down and held out his hand.

'Pass the axe, Johnson. Let me get a feel of

it, see what real work is like.'

The boys laughed again and Johnson passed over the two handed axe.

Hogan held it loosely in his hands and walked up to a massive Oak tree. He stood, legs apart. It felt good in his hands. Right. Three feet of polished Hickory and four pounds of English steel.

He picked a spot on the trunk, drew a deep breath and then took a huge swing.

The bottom half of the trunk simply exploded and a hail of splinters buzzed and whistled through the air like shrapnel. The Hickory handle shattered and the four pound steel head punched its way right through the trunk and embedded itself into the tree behind it. And then, ever so slowly, the immense Oak tree crashed majestically to the ground taking four other trees with it on its way down.

There was a stunned pause, eventually broken by Johnson.

'Gosh. Good strike, sir. Well done.'

The other boys all clapped as if they were watching a good play or perhaps a goal in a soccer match. Hogan raised an eyebrow. It was the first time that he had come across the English Public school ethos. Be polite, be on time and never, ever appear to be taken by surprise. Even if your new guest has just smashed an Oak tree into smithereens with a single blow of an old, blunt axe.

Hogan dropped the remnants of the axe handle to the floor.

'Well that's about that,' he said. 'Load up and let's call it quits for today, boys.'

They walked back in silence again. Hogan on point.

And his body shimmered in the heat haze that boiled off him as he walked.

Chapter 14

The Belmarsh Boys were on the move. After the attack on the American Embassy, their new leader, or the Chief, as he now preferred to be addressed, had finally forced the mob into some semblance of order.

Firstly he chose five personal guards, then he divided the rest of the gang into roughly four groups of fifty each. He had appointed himself some captains and, below them in the hierarchy a group of lieutenants. Each captain controlled a group of fifty and each group of fifty had been split into five groups of ten. In charge of each of these groups was a lieutenant.

Discipline was harsh and absolute. The few men who had not taken well to the new command structure were simply taken to one side and beaten to death by the others.

And now they were traveling out of London, raping and pillaging as they went, feeding off the general population like the Vikings of old. In the front of the column of evil rode the Chief, Basel Ratford. Or, as the pre-pulse newspapers had dubbed him, the Gentleman Killer. It was an odd moniker to attach to a serial killer as he was neither a gentleman, nor did he in fact, ever kill gentlemen. He was an ex-supermarket packer who killed teenage boys, dressed them up in tuxedo and top hat and then, under the cover of night, posed them in various positions in public places to be discovered by the next morning's commuters. He had reached the remarkable tally of nine before a police car ran a red light and smashed into Ratford's car, only to discover a dead, well dressed teenage boy in his trunk.

The police commissioner had tried to spin the story to make it appear like good police work, however the tabloids had run with it under the headline, 'Keystone cops smash Killer case…literally!'

Ratford rode at the front of the column. His men had taken a new Jaguar XJ and stripped the engine out to lighten it. Then they had gone to the Bonny Bridge riding club in Millbrook road, a mere half a mile from the American Embassy, and commandeered a few horses. Two of these horses were harnessed via saddle harnesses to a pair of D-rings that had been hammered into the Jag's coachwork. Then the front windshield had been smashed out and two drivers sat in the front two seats, one to control the horse's reins and the other to steer. The Commander in Chief sat on a leather 'La-Z-boy' recliner that had been strapped to the roof of the car.

Behind him, being drawn by another two horses, was an open back Volvo truck, piled high with supplies. But this seemingly huge pile of food and consumables was not nearly enough for all two hundred men, so scavenging was a constant need.

From a distance the column looked like a carnival. The ex-cons had helped themselves to whatever clothes they had wanted from the very best shops in London and had given full rein to their sartorial whims.

Full length fur coats from Harrods. Men wearing women's felt pillbox hats with long pheasant feathers from Rachel Morgan; milliners to the Queen. Savile Row suits with the arms ripped off to cater for massive, prison-grown biceps. Gold chains and Raybans, Duchamp neckties worn as headbands and bright yellow Louis Vuittion shoes.

Chief Ratford had instituted a few strict rules, the major one being that every likely looking house or person had to be searched for food, water, drink, or drugs and weapons. Any of the aforementioned discovered were to be loaded into the back of the Volvo truck for fair distribution by the captains. As a result of this, the horde swept through the surrounding environs like a massive swarm of *Schistocerca gregaria* or the African desert locust.

The horde had lucked out earlier on that week when, using the weapons that they had, they had stormed the Sportsman Gun Center in Stephendale. Now every member had a firearm of some sort. Mainly double barreled shotguns but also a smattering of hunting rifles and 22 rimfire semi-auto rifles. They had also taken thousands of rounds of ammunition.

Already there had been a number of deaths through accidental discharges. But the commander didn't mind that. He deemed it the result of natural high spirits.

They had left the larger London area some two days ago and the Chief had decided to take them due North, keeping off the major roads in the belief that there would be more food available in the outlying villages.

So far he had been correct and the first small village that they had come to, Moat Wood, although half deserted, had provided fair pickings. The villagers had organized themselves a committee and had pooled all of their remaining food and water in the town hall. This was guarded by two men with shotguns

The horde had rolled over the village in the same manner that Hitler rolled over Poland. Fast and savage, they left no survivors and burned most of the village to the ground.

Today, however, the Chief was looking for bigger bounty. He had sent two horse riding scouts ahead and one had just returned.

He trotted up to the chief and threw out a perfect Nazi salute.

'Chief!'

The Chief nodded. 'Talk to me.'

'Village about five miles ahead, Chief. Judge's Hill. It's on a cross road, got a stream running through. The residents have barricaded the roads. Proper ones, not just piles of furniture. There's wood fencing and cars parked against it. Guards looking over the top. Armed. Shotguns and rifles.'

The Chief nodded. Pleased. He beckoned to one of his captains who came running over.

'Captain,' said the Chief. 'Make sure that all of the boys have ammunition. We're going shopping.'

***

Five miles away, a young girl pulled her horse to a halt outside a barricade made by two Landrovers that had been pushed across a gap in a fence to form a gate. Four men pushed them open and she rode through as they closed behind her.

She trotted down the narrow road and stopped in front of a large Georgian house. She jumped from the saddle and simply left the horse. The animal stood still and cropped at the short lawn as the girl ran up the steps, opened the door and went to the first room on the right.

'Axel,' she greeted as she walked in.

A young man looked up from the desk that he and two other men were standing over. All three men were dressed in identical No. 4 warm weather service dress of the Queen's Royal Surrey Regiment. They all had three captains' stars on their epaulettes.

'Jenny,' he replied. 'How goes?'

'Not good,' she glanced at the two other young men and greeted them before she answered Axel. 'Patrick, Dom.' They nodded their acceptance. 'That band of nut cases is close and heading our way. Probably five miles out or so.'

'Are you sure?' Asked Axel. 'Definitely heading this way?'

Jenny nodded. 'Definitely, brother mine.'

Axel stood up straight. 'Well, gentlemen,' he said. 'Looks like the time has come. Sound the general alert and let's get to it.'

Both Patrick and Dom left the room and, less than a minute later, the banshee like howl of an old Second World War air raid siren shattered the clear English air.

Axel and his two friends, all captains in Queen's Royal Surrey Regiment, had been rotated out of the endless Afghanistan war and sent home for three weeks R&R. Axel had invited the other two for a week at his father's house in the country where they would ride and shoot grouse and drink until the early hours. His younger sister, Jenny, was also there although his parents had stayed on at their townhouse in London.

The first night that they arrived the pulse hit. Within two hours the three officers knew what had happened, although they all thought that it had been the result of a low level nuclear strike as opposed to a natural event. The three of them had immediately donned their uniforms in order to help impart a measure of authority to what they were about to do. They then called on the local priest, the local councilor, the head of the village Rotary Club and the president of the village Women's Institute and insisted on a meeting at Judge Hall, Axel's father's house.

The three soldiers had explained what a pulse was and the inevitable outcomes. They put forward a plan to fortify the village, pool recourses and start a militia. They did not brook any arguments. As a result of their meticulous planning and the backing of the village noteworthies, they had erected a ten-foot fence around the entire village within three days. This fence had been constructed from material pillaged from fences in the interior of the walled area, Then it was fortified with earthen embankments and had a walkway six foot up to provide sentries with a good vantage point from which to see and to fire.

They had then collected all of the firearms and ammunition in the district and surrounds and put the priest in charge of the armory. The food was taken to the village hall and the Women's Institute was put in charge of that. The local doctor and nurse were deemed to be in charge of all medicines and care.

Axel had then taken all of the able bodied men, of which there were one hundred and fifty, and organized them into fifteen groups of ten. For no other reason than it was easy to do, he then put one of each of the local rugby team, into each group and designated them, Team Leader. These fifteen Team Leaders reported directly to him, Patrick and Dom. The groups were then put into three groups of five teams, the idea being that each group would spend eight hours on watch out of every twenty four with the second group being on standby as the third group slept.

All told there were thirty-six weapons of various vintage and caliber. Enough to arm the watch group and the standby group plus the three officers. The weapons consisted mainly of 12 gauge double barreled shotguns although there were two first world war Webley revolvers with a surprising amount of ammunition (some one hundred rounds), owned by the ninety-four year old mister Sturgeon who was partially blind and almost wholly deaf. However, mister Sturgeon absolutely refused to relinquish both revolvers arguing that, if push came to shove it would be left to him to sort the whole mess out.

Axel had taken the second revolver and eighty rounds of ammunition. He had also taken one of the two pump-action shotguns that they had found. Patrick took the other.

Dom opted for a Savage model 11 hunting rifle in a 308 Winchester round with a four plus one box magazine. Dom had also found a two-handed broadsword in the village hall that he had strapped to his back. But then, that was Dom for you. The rest of the weapons were handed out on an ad hoc basis.

The British soldiers did not stop there. Firstly, Axel instituted a series of long sweep patrols, on horseback, to ensure that anything that was happening within twenty miles of the village was reported and planned for and, secondly, he and his two friends started putting in more defenses.

They used the villagers to dig a series of wide shallow ditches, not to stop, merely to impede any charge of people or horses. Then they stripped the hardware store of all of its steel nails over one inch in length. They took the nails to the local blacksmith who, with the help of a veritable crowd of villagers, soldered them together in sets of two. Each nail was then bent at an opposite ninety-degree angle to form a caltrop. Basically, an anti-personnel weapon that always lands with one spike facing up when thrown onto the ground. The blacksmith churned out over ten thousand of these and Axel got the villagers to spread them liberally around the approaches, particularly in the shallow ditches.

Finally, the three officers collected all of the large kitchen knives, carvers, chefs' knives and so on, as well as all of the broom handles in the village. Then, using a knife, a broom handle and a length of duct tape, they fashioned a rudimentary but deadly spear for all of those who did not have firearms.

All of these precautions had been implemented in order to prevent roving gangs of outsiders draining the meager stocks of the village. All newcomers were turned away unless they were returning residents or blood relatives of current villagers. However, the soldiers were under no illusions and knew that their defenses could most likely be breached by a determined force of over two hundred armed desperados.

'So,' said Dom. 'When do you think that they'll get here?'

Axel shrugged. 'Can't be one hundred percent sure. If it were me, then I would camp up a mile or so away. It's getting late. Then I'd hit us at first light or just before.'

'Makes sense,' agreed Dom.

'What do you rate our chances?' Asked Patrick.

'Zero to none,' answered Axel. 'Can't see us keeping them out for more than a day. We're outnumbered, outgunned and the perimeters too large.'

'What about evacuating?' Suggested Patrick.

Axel shook his head. 'Already spoken about that to all of the worthies. The general consensus seems to be, here we stand. I tend to agree. We all know what it's like out there. One could run for now but not forever.'

'My God,' said Dom. 'What I'd give to have ten fully armed chaps from the regiment with us. Now that would be a no-brainer.'

Axel chuckled. 'Yep, we'd win for sure. Pity.'

'I notice that your father keeps a particularly well stocked wine cellar,' ventured Patrick. 'I think that I spied upon a magnum of Chateau Lafite Rothschild 2009. Do you think he'd be awfully peeved if we guzzled that down?'

'Course not,' answered Axel. 'What's a thirty thousand dollar bottle of wine between friends? Anyway,' he continued. 'You only live once.'

'True,' agreed Dom. 'And sometimes not even that long.'

They laughed and headed for the wine cellar.

Chapter 15

Sam crawled out of the cupboard below the stairs. He was hungry but still had water. Surprisingly, his diet of dry dog food was supplying him with enough calories and vitamins to keep him alert. It was merely the awful taste and consistency that was causing his hunger.

And, by now, the body of his mother had putrefied and the stench was appalling. He decided that it was time to move on. First he went upstairs and found his scout rucksack. Into this he put a wooly jumper, spare socks and underwear, an extra shirt and a pair of shorts and a sleeping bag. Then he thought for a while. He rummaged through his father's bedside table and found a Swiss army knife with about a million blades on it. Also a plastic cigarette lighter. After that he went to the medicine cabinet in the bathroom. He knew that people needed medicine but he had no idea what medicine was for what. He spent a while reading labels and thinking, his face serious. Eventually he settled on a box of something called Ibuprofen and a large container of a drug that the doctor had recently prescribed to his mother. Amoxillin broad-spectrum antibiotics. He followed these with a box of various size bandages and a bottle of Dettol antiseptic. On the way out he picked up the rest of the dog biscuits and two bottles of lemonade that were hidden in his cupboard.

He left via the front door, which he left open, and walked out, staggering slightly under the weight of the full rucksack. He had no idea where he was going; he simply felt that he needed to be somewhere else. After a while he left the road and walked close to the hedges and shrubs. He wasn't sure why but he thought that he had better be as inconspicuous as possible.

He walked until the sun went down, eventually stopping because he could no longer see. He burrowed into a thick hedge, unrolled his sleeping bag, crawled in and fell into an exhausted sleep.

Above him the sky glowed with all the colors of the rainbow as the sun continued to pulse and flare.

Chapter 16

Seth Hil-Nu lay on his camp bed, arms by his side. He had fasted for three days and, after intense meditation, had now entered the objectless stage of existence having passed through gross, subtle, bliss and I-ness stages. He was now part of the vast stillness of the universe.

And through the vastness of forever he wandered, letting the pull of the Life-Light find him. He knew that Ammon had placed a guard outside his tent so that he would not be disturbed. So he lay. For two days he traveled the cosmic infinite, encompassing his spirit in a protective ball of Life-Light, speeding through time and space like a comet.

On the third day, all around him coalesced into a pageant of light and sound and he opened his eyes to find himself hovering above a world of blue and green. He let the Life-Light take him closer. And closer.

Suddenly the air around him was torn apart with explosions of fire. He allowed the Life-Light to keep him away from danger and he concentrated, letting his mind meld with the creatures below.

What he heard he did not understand. Phrases flashed through his mind. February the 25th, 1942. Unidentified Flying Object. Anti-aircraft battery. German aircraft. Japanese bombers.

And then he was gone. At peace. Wandering again. Crossing the barriers of time and space. Encapsulated in Life-Light.

The same blue-green planet. In the sky below him some sort of animal. Bird? Massive. No, not bird. Mechanical. He melded. June 18th, 1963. Look…an unidentified flying object of some sort. A ball of light, maybe a flying saucer. Air traffic control. Can you see this? Can you frigging see this?

Peace. Traveling again. The forth day of meditation and voyaging.

Buildings. Some sort of homestead. A farm. Seth drifted down. Closer. A door opens and two beings walk out. One dark skinned, one light. They see him. He melds. They are called Betty and Barney Hill. He can feel their fear. He wipes their memories. But they are a species that he has never worked with before and the memory wipe doesn't take properly. Instead they are left with a mélange of fact and fiction. For the rest of their lives they claim to have been abducted by gray-skinned aliens from the Zeta Reticuli star system.

He leaves. The Life-Light is close. He realizes that he is now traveling only through time and no longer space.

Power surges through him. Heady and exhilarating. All around him the Life-Light coalesces and separates. Swirling and diving. Its beauty is indescribable. But he cannot use its full power, as he is not actually there. He is still in his body, in a campaign tent in another time and place. But, even in his diminished state, he can garner enough power to do what he needs to.

He sinks closer to the surface of the planet. A city. Massive beyond belief. Buildings as tall as mountains. Many of them are burning. Sentient beings, the same ones that he has seen before, walking down the roads in their thousands. It looks to be some manner of evacuation. Are they fleeing a war? Disease? He melds. But all that he gets is fear. Panic. The end of days. Such is the collective horror that it scalds his mind and he withdraws.

For a while longer he revels in the Life-Light. He absorbs it, for the Life-Light is strong in this time and place. And he marks well both the time and place, for the Life-Light is all important. Nothing else matters.

Moments later he is awake in his tent. Elated. He now has a way to save his people. The Fair-Folk will persevere. He has found a place for them to go.

Chapter 17

Nathaniel had been busy. Over the last week or so, he and the boys had cleared the trees back from the walls. They had then cut off all branches between two and three inches thick, sharpened both ends and dug in a forest of spikes around the walls and the gate.

The Marine had then taken the fishing line that Conradie had supplied and set up a rudimentary alarm system. Trip lines attached to tin cans filled with stones. Kick the line and the can would rattle. Simple but effective. He had also instituted a twenty four hour watch so that at least four armed people were on the walls at all times.

The Professor had found a stash of cigarettes in the matron's room and, as she had gone on leave before the pulse, he gave them to Nathaniel. They were Silk Cut, so mild as to be akin to smoking soap bubbles. Hogan pulled the filters off and they became marginally more acceptable.

He was smoking one at the moment, sitting on a wooden bench in the middle of the quadrangle and watching the smoke spiral lazily up into the still, late, afternoon air. The English sun was low and feeble, the rays washing the foliage of the surrounding forest with subtle yellows and oranges. The multicolored aurora of the now almost constant solar flares rippled silently across the skies. Its soundless beauty taking with it thousands of years of mankind's most scientific achievements.

The Marine sensed someone approaching.

'Mind if I join you?' Asked the Prof.

Nathaniel said nothing. Merely gestured at the empty side of the bench.

'Penny for your thoughts.'

Hogan smiled and pointed at the sky. 'It's beautiful.'

'Yes,' agreed the Prof. 'But evil is oft the author of beauty.'

Nathaniel shook his head. 'It's not evil. It's merely light. Gamma rays. A thing. All that it has done is to expose us, humanity, for what we are. That light up there has shone into our dark places and shown us that evil is merely a point of view. It is unspectacular, it is human and it sits at our tables and shares our beds. It is us.'

'Very philosophical, Master Gunnery Sergeant.'

Nathaniel shrugged. 'I am a soldier. People think that soldiers spend their time fighting. That's not true. Soldiers spend their time waiting to fight and, on the whole, hoping that they never have to. Soldiers spend most of their time wondering what the hell it's all about. Philosopher? No, not that. Thinker? Perhaps. Are you a religious man, Prof?'

The older man shook his head. 'I am a man of science. Empirical proof. Evidence thrice checked and checked again.'

Hogan grinned. 'That's irrational, Prof. If you cannot prove that something exists, well, then you also can't prove that it doesn't exist.'

'I'm not one to let rationality stand in the way of a good theory,' laughed the Professor. 'So, good soldier,' he continued. 'The defenses are all up to scratch. What do we do next?'

Nathaniel took a drag. Exhaled. Stared at the glowing tip. 'It won't be long now and a few things are going to happen. Firstly, survivors, singles and groups, will begin to appear at the gates. You will have to decide on whether you let any of them in or if you simply tell them to piss off and die.'

The Prof looked uncomfortable. 'Can't you make those sort of decisions?'

'No. I won't be here forever. I need to keep heading north. Please don't ask me why because I have no idea. I just feel that I need to. It's a compulsion, like birds flying to the sun. But it's pretty simple; you need to let in anyone with skills or resources that you need. Doctors, nurses, anyone with livestock, supplies.'

'And all others we sentence to death?' Asked the Prof.

'Not necessarily,' rejoined Nathaniel. 'You merely send them on their way. Too many people and this place will become unsustainable. However, you are also going to get larger groups that will insist. Armed groups. Maybe even ex-soldiers. Policemen. You will have to deal with them most harshly. Show no quarter. Give no warning.'

'I'm not sure that I understand,' said the Professor.

'I mean that you must kill them. Open fire on them as soon as it looks as though they may try to force their way in. Cut them down to the last man.'

'Well,' said the Prof. 'We shall cross that bridge when we come to it.'

'No,' disagreed the Marine. 'You shall cross that bridge now. Everyone. The teachers, the scholars. Everyone must be told that when, not if, when you are attacked, the attackers must be repelled at all costs. No one can afford to hold back. People must shoot to kill and they must continue to shoot until the enemy is no more. I cannot stress this enough, Professor.'

'They're a good bunch of chaps,' said the Professor. 'When push comes to shove they will do their duty.'

Nathaniel took out another cigarette. Ripped the filter off. Placed the cancer stick into his mouth and lit. 'There was a guy, US army general. Did some studies. Did you know that, in the Second World War, only fifteen to twenty percent of soldiers actually fired at the enemy. One in every five. Those who would not fire did not run or hide - in many cases they were willing to risk greater danger to rescue comrades, get ammunition, or run messages. They simply would not fire their weapons at the enemy, even when faced with repeated waves of banzai charges.

Why did these men fail to fire? I'll tell you why, Professor, the simple and demonstrable fact is that there is, within most men and women, an intense resistance to killing other people. A resistance so strong that, in many circumstances, soldiers on the battlefield will die before they can overcome it.'

Nathaniel took a drag. 'Do yourself and your community a favor, Prof. Talk to the boys. And the girls. Kill or die. Tell them that, over and over again. Kill or die. Kill or die. Kill…or…die.'

The Prof rubbed his eyes with the heels of his hands. Then he sighed. A sound of absolute exhaustion. For the first time Nathaniel saw how close the older man was to collapse. An academic suited more to classrooms and civic dinners, as opposed to telling a bunch of teenagers that they had to kill their fellow man in order to survive.

Nathaniel put his hand on the Prof's shoulder. 'Sorry,' he said. 'I know that things are tough. Why don't you get some vittles and take an early night. Tomorrow…well, I won't bullshine you, tomorrow things will be just as bad, but you'll be more rested.'

The Professor took a deep breath. 'O sleep! O gentle sleep! Nature's soft nurse, how have I frighted thee, That thou no more wilt weigh my eyelids down

And steep my senses in forgetfulness? Why rather, sleep, liest thou in smoky cribs,

Upon uneasy pallets stretching thee, And hush'd with buzzing night-flies to thy slumber, Than in the perfum'd chambers of the great, Under the canopies of costly state, And lull'd with sound of sweetest melody?'

'Shakespeare?' Asked Nathaniel.

'Yes. Henry the fifth. It's an affectation that one gets, being a scholar in England. We tend to nurture pretension and there is little more pretentious than sprouting the bard.'

'I dunno,' disagreed the Marine. 'I think that it's pretty cool. Better than quoting Walt Disney. Or Garfield.'

'True,' said the Prof. 'However, before I go, good Marine, what else to do?'

'You're going to have to set up some sort of formal command structure. Who takes over if you kick the big one or get injured? And make sure that it's not Conradie. That dude couldn't organize a party in a brewery. I would say one of the older boys, but it's your call. And not only your replacement. You need to put a couple of people in with the nurse to learn what she knows. You need a system of repair and maintenance set up. Someone needs to be in charge of the weapons and the people that are going to be using them. Also, you have an extensive library, get a few scholars to start doing research; natural replacement for drugs, antibiotics, pain killers and such. You have around five thousand rounds of ammunition. Sounds like a lot but it won't last forever. Get someone onto making bows and arrows. Perhaps crossbows, slings, spears, pikes. Send out search parties and see if you can acquire some horses, use force if necessary…'

The Prof held up a hand. 'Enough for now, Nathaniel. I think that I shall take your advice, get a little sustenance and retire for the night.'

He stood up and offered his hand. Nathaniel shook it.

'Thank you, friend.' said the older man. 'Thank you very much.'

Nathaniel finished his cigarette and then sat alone until the sun went down and the moon, three quarter full, rose bright and clear, shining through the collage of color formed by the aurora.

He smelt her fragrance before he heard her. Floral. Fresh cotton. Citrus.

She sat down next to him without asking.

'Maggie,' he greeted.

'Nathaniel,' she answered.

He took out his pack and offered. She shook her head. 'I'll share one, if you don't mind,' she said. 'One or two puffs is about my limit.'

Hogan lit and offered. Maggie took a small drag. The smoke drifted from her mouth. Moonlight white against pale skin. Lips a deep pink. Highlights of lunar-blue woven through the strands of her copper and golden hair.

'What was London like?' She asked the Marine.

He hesitated before he answered. Remembering the Professor telling him that Maggie's parents lived in the city.

'The truth,' she said, sensing his hesitance.

'It's bad,' he said. 'Very bad. Worse than one could ever imagine. Where about did your folks live?'

'Central. The Barbican. Right in the middle.'

'Were they young, old, fit, healthy?'

Maggie shook her head. 'I'm an only child. Born late to parents who had long since given up any idea of having children. It was my father's second marriage. My mother is twenty years younger than him. He's almost eighty now. Pills for high blood pressure, statins for cholesterol, type 2 diabetes.'

Nathaniel raised an eyebrow. 'Maggie, what can I say that you don't already know. I'm sorry. Sometimes life sucks.'

He glanced sideways at the girl. A single tear rolled down her cheek. The moonlight turned it into a tiny rivulet of blue ice against her soft pale skin. The Marine said nothing. Uncomfortable with emotions. Trained to kill, not to empathize. Eventually he spoke.

'Hey, you know, I grew up in a town called Toad Suck, Arkansas?'

Maggie giggled. 'Toad Suck?'

'Yep. Toad Suck, Perry County, Arkansas. Home of the famous Toad Suck Daze music festival. Population some 60 000. The Hogans have been Toad Suckers for five generations. Been sucking for over two hundred years.'

The girl laughed out loud. 'You made that up.'

Nathaniel shook his head. 'No ways. We had a big old double story house on Ira Gill Lane. My daddy ran the Arkansas Pet & People photography barn. My mom did charity work for the Toad Suck Daze festival. Had two sisters, Charlene and Bethany. Both older than me. Both married Toad Suckers.'

Maggie sighed. 'You talk in the past tense.'

'I do, Maggie.'

'That's sad.'

'Yep.' Nathaniel pulled on his cigarette.

Maggie lent against him, her hair spilling onto his shoulder, filling his nostrils with her fragrance.

'I'm eighteen years old,' she said.

'Oh,' responded Nathaniel. Not sure what the girl was talking about.

She looked up at the Marine. 'So, I'm not a child.'

Nathaniel nodded, not trusting his voice.

Maggie stood up and held out her hand. 'Take me to your room, Marine.'

The two of them walked, hand in hand, to Nathaniel's room.

He closed the door behind them, slotting the bolt into place.

Nathaniel sat on the edge of his bed, pulled his boots and socks off then stood up to remove the rest of his clothes. Maggie also disrobed in an unselfconscious way, folding her cotton dress neatly over the chair in the room. She wasn't wearing a bra and her breasts were small, firm. The nipples thrown into stark relief by the silver lunar light pouring in through the window. She put her arms around the Marine's neck and, even though she was a tall girl she still had to stand on tiptoes to reach.

They kissed for a while. Softly. Hesitant. Then Nathaniel picked her up. Easily. As if she weighed nothing. And he laid her on the bed. She lifted her hips and, using her thumb, hitched her panties down over her ankles, tossing them onto the floor.

Nathaniel looked at her for a while. Marveling in the soft smoothness of her skin. The exquisite paleness of it, frosted by the merest hint of freckles scattered across her chest like tiny flakes of gold.

He knelt over her and they kissed again, this time a little more urgently. And then she grasped him by his shoulders and pushed him down. Insistent, her breath faster now, urgent, her hips rising up to meet his mouth. Her fingers entwined in his hair, tugging, adamant. Her need a desperate necessity. A break from reality. Then she cried out as all feeling culminated in an ecstasy of fulfillment.

And Nathaniel moved up and entered her. Their lovemaking an affirmation of life in a new world of dissolution and bereavement.

Chapter 18

Seth spent the next few days researching the blue green planet. He traveled both geographically and horologically, spreading his research through time in order to get a feel of the history of the beings that dwelled there.

He studied them from both close and far. At times even meeting them. On the whole they would retain little or no memory of him as he became more and more skilled at wiping their memories. But they were a willful species and remembered far more about the little gray men from far away than he would have believed.

After spending a total of nine days in meditational stasis, he returned, ready to report to commander Ammon.

Seth sat on the edge of his bed, sipping a cocktail of distilled mead, milk and honey. Replacing the fluids and energy that he had used up whilst traveling. Commander Ammon sat on a hide-covered stool opposite the mage.

'It is a world similar to ours,' said Seth. 'However, there is much more land. Whereas we have but a few islands they have vast swathes of fertile soil. Thousands of square leagues. I have chosen a particular place that is strong in magiks. An ancient place called Cornwall in a land called England'

'And will they accept us as refugees?'

Seth shook his large gray head. 'No. They are an unbelievably war-like people. Since time immemorial they have fought amongst themselves.'

'Large wars?' Enquired the commander.

'Beyond our imagining. Weapons of mass destruction that make our most powerful magiks pale into nothingness. In my travels I saw entire cities leveled by weapons capable of unleashing storms of fire that competed against the very sun itself. Hand held weapons that can kill over many leagues distance. I saw vast prisons that were there for no other purpose than to exterminate the beings that were imprisoned there. Exterminate them in their millions.'

'So then,' said Ammon. 'There is no point in going. It would be the old cliché of jumping from the cooking pot only to land in the fire.'

'No, not at all,' disagreed Seth. 'Let me finish. I am telling you of their past. What they once were.'

'Ah,' interrupted Ammon. 'They have progressed. They have learned the value of life?'

'The opposite,' said Seth. 'Somehow, and I know not why, they have regressed. The flying machines no longer work. Their mechanical modes of transport. Their massive night-lights. None of it works anymore. It is as though the gods have abandoned them, taking with them all knowledge of the past and leaving them as cave dwellers in a broken palace. As a result they are a dying race. Hundreds of thousands of them perish every day. And those not dying of natural causes are being killed by the stronger ones. They are barbaric beyond belief.'

'And their magiks?' Asked the commander.

'They no longer seem to have any,' answered Seth.

'It is almost too good to be true. Can you take me there?'

Seth nodded. 'I have much power. The Life-Light there is so strong that, even in my corporeal form, I managed to fill myself with it. Let me finish my potion and I will oblige.'

The mage continued to sip his nourishing cocktail, not rushing. Ammon sat still and waited. Patiently.

'Right,' said Seth. 'Come and sit next to me. We shall join hands and travel. I must be honest and warn you; this will be a little uncomfortable to you. The disassociation of soul from self can be very disturbing for the uninitiated. But I shall be with you so there is little to worry about. Just remember, do not panic. Breathe deeply and slowly and, relax. Ready?'

Ammon joined hands and nodded. 'Ready.'

The universe stretched thin. Ammon felt as though his brain had been siphoned out of his cranium and liquidized. Pain scoured his mind like spiders scrabbling on a tiled surface. Light filled his being and exploded. Then all was dark.

'Commander,' said Seth. 'Open your eyes.'

Ammon did so. He lay on his back on a field of rough grass. Above him the sky was filled with the multicolor of the Life-Light. The air was thick and frigid. Heady. His head still buzzed with pain.

'You mendacious double-dealer,' he accused Seth. 'A little uncomfortable?'

The mage laughed. A dry staccato sound. Like the breaking of twigs. 'Well, if I told the truth would you have come?'

Ammon rubbed his large forehead. 'Probably. Not sure.'

'Now, my friend,' warned Seth. 'You must remember. You are not here but you are here at the same time. Your physical body sits in stasis in my campaign tent but your inner self has traveled. However, any harm that you incur here will be carried over to your corporeal being. In other words, you die here, you die for real.'

Ammon stared around. The land was flat and windswept. And as he turned and looked, he saw them. Stones, perhaps six to ten feet high. Standing in a circle around him. Maybe twenty of them. He felt a shiver of fear run through him.

'Ley stones,' he said, his voice raw with horror.

'Yes,' agreed Seth. His voice calm.

'But you said that they had no magik. These stones show that they still practice the old ways. The way of the druids. You idiot, Seth. You have lead us into destruction.' Ammon was literally shaking in terror.

'No,' said Seth. 'Stop. Relax. Feel. Just feel with your mind. Let your thoughts flow.'

Ammon stood still for a while. 'You're correct,' he eventually said. 'Nothing. These stones must be very, very old. The magik has long since gone from them. They must have forgotten how to control the power.' He turned to face Seth and bowed slightly. 'I offer my apologies, friend. You did warn me not to panic.'

Seth's dry laugh cracked out again. 'No need to apologize,' he said. 'The first time that I landed in them I literally almost soiled myself, so you have done yourself proud to maintain your dignity to the extent that you did. However, as you know, these stones would only be placed in an area of great power. So, this will be our staging post. This is the place known as Cornwall and it is here where I shall form the gateway to bring our people through. It is isolated from the beings that dwell on this planet, there is ample water and, as you can see, large open spaces. Perfect.'

Seth looked at the commander, waiting for comment. But Ammon was staring out across the plain. Approaching from afar was a small, hairy, four-legged beast, running at full pelt. Its oddly long tongue dangled from the side of its mouth and its equally oddly long ears flapped behind its head. Ammon tensed and prepared to defend himself.

'Oh, don't worry about those,' assured Seth as the beast drew closer. 'They are called Dogs. It probably just wants to lick you.'

'Lick me?' Asked Ammon in horror. 'Why?'

'Best that I can figure out is that the male beings that live on this planet have bred these animals to be their companions. Their, best friends, as it were. And, as far as I can see, being licked donates the dog's friendship.'

True to form the dog, a Red Setter, desperate for company now that its master and his friends had all left, ran up to Ammon and licked his face in greeting. The commander let his mind flow into the dog.

'Love,' he said to Seth. 'This dog thing seems to have only two or three rudimentary thoughts; food, water and love.'

'Yes,' agreed Seth. 'They have a saying here; a Dog is a man's best friend.'

'I see. And what about the females of the species?'

Seth looked puzzled. 'Odd as it may sound, from the little research that I have managed, it appears that gemstones are a female's best friend. I believe the saying goes; diamonds are a girl's best friend.'

'How do I stop this animal licking me?' Asked the commander.

'Tell him to sit,' responded Seth. 'They are very obedient.'

'Sit,' commanded Ammon.

The dog sat, tongue lolling out. Waiting for its next command.

'Very interesting.'

'Yes,' agreed Seth. 'You have to be a little careful of them. Sometimes they try to bite you. And their teeth are formidable.'

'Why?' Asked Ammon. 'I thought that they were my best friend.'

'You are,' said Seth. 'But they can still bite you.'

Ammon shook his head. 'What a strange planet this is. I feel that we will be able to improve things a great deal here when we arrive. I feel that some sort of order wouldn't go amiss. No, not at all.'

'I agree, commander. Now, should we link hands and return?'

The two fair folk joined hands. Seth concentrated. Light shimmered and they were gone.

The dog lay down and whined for a while.

Chapter 19

Axel had been correct about one thing. The Belmarsh boys approached at first light the next morning. However, they did not attack. They simply massed about four hundred yards from the one wall and stood there.

Eventually a man came forward, riding a horse.

He rode to within three hundred yards and then stopped and stood up in his stirrups.

'Hooeee!' He yelled. 'I need to talk to your leader.'

Patrick nudged Axel who stood up. 'Talk.'

'We will give you an hour to vacate the village. You must leave your weapons, food, drugs and any other supplies. If we see you taking anything we will attack you.'

'No,' retaliated Axel. 'We leave without anything and we will all starve. Or worse.'

'This is a non-repeatable, once only offer,' shouted the man on horseback. 'I advise that you take it now. You have a minute to comply and after that…you will all be dead before the sun goes down.'

Axel shook his head to himself. All that the thugs wanted was an easy way to get the villagers disarmed and out into the open. And there was no way that was going to happen. He wondered if he should play for time and then realized – what was the point? He made his decision.

'Dom.'

'Yup.'

'You reckon that you can take the guy on horseback?'

'With my eyes closed,' assured Dom.

'Do it then.'

Dom brought the rifle up to his eye, slipped the safety off, drew a breath. Let it out slowly. And fired.

The criminal flipped off the back of his horse like he had been swept up by a giant hand. Dom worked the bolt and drew a bead on a man sitting in a chair on top of a car. But as he fired the man jumped. The high velocity bullet clipped his heel as he went over, spraying blood in a puff of crimson mist. His howl of agony was clear from where they stood. Dom kept at it, firing three more times and knocking down two more criminals.

'Steady!' Shouted Axel, waving his hand at the villagers so that they kept down. 'Stay as you are.'

Dom reloaded his rifle with five more rounds. Beside him there were another three rifles amongst the villagers. Axel had ensured that they were the best shots. He would use them first, keeping the shotguns and sidearms until the enemy were really close. Perhaps twenty yards.

The Belmarsh boys were milling around at the moment. Confused at the way things had gone. Then there was a bellow from their commander and, almost as one, the two hundred plus criminals charged the village, screaming and firing as they came.

The first shallow, caltrop-strewn ditch was a classic example of low-tech antipersonnel installments. The leading row of criminals leapt into the ditch and the steel caltrops punched through the soles of their shoes and boots. But more thugs were piling into the ditch behind them forcing them forward so that they fell onto more caltrops which punched into their exposed chests and faces. The second wave tripped over the fallen first wave and, as they crawled forward they too became victims of the deadly sharpened steel traps. There was a general cry of dismay as the third wave clambered over the trench merely to be met with a field so liberally strewn with spiked metal caltrops that it was impossible not to step on one.

'Rifles!' Shouted Axel. 'Fire at will. Pick your targets.'

The four rifles opened up. Slow. Methodical. Each target aimed at and hit.

The Belmarsh charge reversed and became a rout.

Chapter 20

Sam crawled out from his sleeping bag, rolled it up and crammed it into his rucksack. Then he took out one of the bottles of lemonade and took a few sips. The bubbles fizzed in his mouth and went up his nose making him sneeze.

'Oh-ho,' he heard someone say. 'What have we here? Some sort of sneezing animal I venture to say.'

He shrank back into the hedge, trying to make himself as small as possible. And then a terrible beast with huge teeth and massive snorting nostrils pushed its head into the hedge and stared at him.

Sam screamed. High pitched and formless as the build up of terror over the last few days was released in one ragged emotional outburst. The beast snorted and pulled away to be replaced by a man's face. Ruddy and covered in a large black beard. Eyes a bright shiny blue and eyebrows the size of hamsters.

'Steady there, boy. There's nothing to fear here. That merely be Dancer, my old horse. She just be curious, that's all.'

Sam was frozen to the spot, shaking, his eyes wide in stark horror.

The man's face disappeared and Sam heard him call out.

'Mama,' he called. 'Come over here and be smart about it. There's a wee chiseler in the bushes and he be right scared.'

Within seconds a female face showed itself to Sam. An older woman. Smooth skin, long gray hair in two plaits, one on either side of her head. She had the same unsettlingly blue eyes as the old man and she radiated a calm kindness.

Sam relaxed and then he held his arms out to her. She grabbed him under his arms and lifted him to her, picking him up, his head on her shoulders. She stroked his hair.

'Come on, me wee bairn. Let's to the caravan and get you a lie down and then something hot to eat.'

Sam shook his head. 'Not sleepy.'

'Okay then. Would you like something to eat?'

Sam nodded. 'Hungry. Only had dog biscuits since the bad men killed my mommy.'

'Well, you're with friends now,' the old lady said.

Sam looked up from her shoulder and saw a row of horse drawn caravans. Twenty of them. All painted in bright primary colors.

Seated on the front of each one, reins in hand, was an armed man. In some cases two. Hard looking men, dark skinned, long black hair, beards and moustaches. They all carried assault rifles. A mix of AK's and American M16's. One of them winked at Sam and smiled. His blue eyes twinkled with suppressed mischief. Sam smiled back. For the first time since his mommy had died he felt truly safe.

The old lady put him down but continued to hold his left hand.

'The people call me Mama,' she said to Sam. 'And what do we call you?'

'Sam.'

'A good name. Sam be it then.'

The old man came over and held out his hand. Sam took it and shook it solemnly.

'Well met, young Sam,' said the old man. 'The people call me Papa Dante. I won't bother you with all the others names, you seem to be a bright enough lad so I be sure that you'll pick them up as we go.'

'Are you gypsies?' Asked Sam

'Aye, some may call us that,' answered Papa Dante. 'Though we be not too fond of the calling. We prefer to be called Pavees or even Lucht Siuil, which means The Walking People. Now come along to my vardo and Mama shall give you a mug of soul-warming chicken soup.'

Mama led Sam to the caravan, or vardo, as Papa Dante called it. She pulled down some steps and Sam climbed up. She went up next. Then Papa pulled the steps up, vaulted into the front seat, flicked the reins and Dancer shambled into a slow plodding walk.

Mama took out a thermos flask and poured soup from it into a large clay mug. She handed it to Sam. 'Careful,' she said. 'It's hot.'

The little boy sipped at it cautiously. It was delicious. Thick and unctuous and chickeny. After a week of dried dog biscuits the explosion of flavor literally brought tears of pleasure to his eyes.

'Are you alright?' Asked Mama concernedly.

Sam nodded. 'Nice. Yum. Thank you.' He continued slurping. By the time he had finished the large mug he was full and, although he professed not to be sleepy he had slept little over the last few days, his slumber light and full of fear.

Mama took the empty mug from him and walked him to the back of the vardo. She pulled aside a curtain to reveal a large double bed, thick feather mattress with a down stuffed duvet spread on top.

'Not sleepy,' mumbled Sam.

Mama sat him down, pulled his shoes off, gently pushed him back onto the mattress and covered him with the duvet. He fell asleep almost instantly. She watched him for a while and then went back to her seat beside Papa Dante.

'Poor mite's asleep,' she told her husband.

'Aye, a bit of time in the scratcher will do him the power of good, it shall. Rest and your magical chicken soup, my love. Never more should a man need.'

Mama punched Papa Dante on the arm. 'Sure you be lying you charmer you.' She smiled and leaned up against him.

Softly but clearly, Papa Dante started to sing.

If you ever cross the sea to Ireland
And maybe at the closing of your day
You can seat and watch the sun rise over clada,
And watch the sun go down on Galway bay
Maybe some day I'll go back again to Ireland
If my dear old wife would only pass away,
Now she has my poor old health broke with all her nagging,
And she has a mouth as big as Galway Bay,
After drinking sixteen pints of Arthur Guinness
And she walks down the road with out a sway,
If the auld sea was bare in stead of salty water
A then she would live and die on Galway bay,

After drinking sixteen points in Padgo Murphy
And the bar man say's its time to go,
Now she doesn't try to answer him in Irish
But speaks a language that the Traveller's do not know,
Well on her back she has a map of Ireland,
And when she takes her bath on Saturdays
Well she rubs the care ball soap all round the clada
Just to watch the auld suds go down on Galway bay,
Well her feet are like auld lump of board na Mona
And her hair is like a rake of last years hay,
A and when I rub my around her turage
A she'll forget about auld Galway bay.

The train of caravans continued its progression as the horses clipped and clopped their slow way towards the next place that they were going.

And the hard faced men who guided them scanned the countryside around them and kept their rifles ready to hand.

Chapter 21

Axel had a decision to make. It was time to take a gamble. The first reckless attack by the Belmarsh boys had been repulsed with ease but, Axel was pretty sure, the next attack would take place in a very different fashion.

If he had been in charge of the criminal gang then he would have attacked simultaneously from four sides at once. As long as one attack got through and into the inner defenses then it was game over.

So he split his meager army up into four groups, placing one group on each fence. He ensured that each group had one rifleman and an officer. As there were only three officers, he put the priest in charge of the fourth group. Their orders were simple. The riflemen would start shooting as soon as they saw anyone that they thought they could hit and the shotgunners would wait until the enemy got within twenty yards before opening fire.

He also placed the extra villagers with their makeshift spears on the walls with instructions to stick anyone who came within sticking distance.

The easy initial victory had buoyed the villager's spirits and, although Axel and his fellow officers knew that the victory was almost meaningless, they said nothing to hurt morale.

The second attack happened as Axel had predicted. At a little after three that afternoon the Belmarsh boys charged from four directions at once. But this time their charge was slower. More circumspect as they scanned the ground before them for caltrops and any other nasty surprises that may lie in store.

This slower advance allowed Dom to knock five of them down before they had managed to make more than a dozen yards. When he reloaded and started firing again the group attacking his wall broke and retreated.

Axel's wall also fared well. His rifleman managed to kill one of the opposition but, as soon as they got within fifty yards, Axel opened up with the old Webley, its massive 455 rounds booming out like a cannon complete with fire and smoke. He fired fast and reloaded just as quickly. Within ten seconds he had hit another four criminals and the group retreated.

Patrick's rifleman missed all of his shots and the group charging their wall surged within twenty yards before the volley of shotguns fire forced them back. However, they also returned fire and hit two of the villagers.

It was on the priest's wall that it all went wrong.

Whoever was in charge of the party attacking the priest's wall used a little more common sense than the others and, instead of simply charging will-he-nil-he, he laid down covering fire as his men inched forward. Using fire and movement they edged closer and closer. Every time that a villager popped up to take a shot at them he was greeted with a fusillade of fire, pinning him back down.

They had almost made the wall when the day was saved by, of all people, the ninety four year old mister Sturgeon.

By now the confusion of gunfire and the screams of the wounded had sent mister Sturgeon spiraling back in time to the Second World War. So, he tottered his way to the wall, stepped up onto one of the ramparts and simply started to fire, point blank, into the faces of the attackers.

'Take that, you bastard Nazis,' he shouted. 'Go back to Germany.' After six shots he calmly reloaded and then recommenced firing. The villagers took advantage of this unexpected turn and all opened up at once. Finally the gang members were driven back.

Attack number two repulsed.

'Tonight,' said Axel to himself. 'The next attack will be tonight.'

He took a deep breath. Exhausted.

Chapter 22

It was late afternoon and Papa Dante pulled the vardos off the road and into a field. They unhitched the horses and, by hand, pulled the vardos into a circle or tabor, as Papa Dante called it.

Usually the horses would be hitched to a tree or fence outside of the tabor but, due to circumstances, they were now kept inside the secure circle to prevent theft.

Sam awoke, went to the front of the vardo and looked out. The first thing that he noticed was the children. They had all been riding inside the vardos when Sam had been picked up so he had not seen them. There were over forty of them ranging in age from toddler to young teens. And all of them were hard at work.

Toddlers carrying kindling, bigger kids toting wood logs. Others fetching buckets of water from a nearby stream and yet more grooming the horses. Rubbing them down with hay and then curry combing their coats to a sleek shine.

The women of the clan were laying a group of cooking fires and setting up trestle tables with mugs and plates and various sized bottles.

Some of the men helped to carry heavy items, bags of oats for the horses or large cast iron cooking pots, but, on the whole, the men stood watch. Their blue eyes constantly scanning their surrounds, rifles held ready.

Papa Dante was everywhere. Helping, chiding, laughing and commanding. He glanced up and saw Sam watching so he beckoned to him to come over.

The young boy climbed down and walked to him.

'Sam the man,' bellowed Papa Dante. 'Meet some of the chilluns.'

Papa reeled off a gaggle of Celtic names, talking fast, like an American tobacco auctioneer. 'Dylan, Oisin, Keeva, Siobhan, Keraney, Tierney, Shamus, Ultan.'

There was a chorus of greetings.

'Now, Sam,' continued Papa. 'You go with Keeva and Dylan and collect more wood for the fires. Hurry off now.'

Keeva, a blonde girl of around seven grabbed Sam's hand. 'Come on, you be with us now.' The little girl led the way, tugging Sam along with her. Dylan, a tall twelve year old, walked behind them. Another dark haired, blue-eyed male, hovering on the edge of becoming a man.

'So,' said Keeva. 'Where's your mam and your da?'

'My dad went to work and never came home,' answered Sam. 'Then the bad men came and made my mommy dead. Then I had dog biscuits and then Papa Dante found me in a hedge.'

'Oh. That's sad,' said Keeva, her feelings genuine but shallow as only a child's can be. 'But now that you with us you got lots of ma's and da's. Papa Dante and Mama are the pa and ma for everyone. Even the big ones.'

'They're not the ma and da of Gogo,' said Dylan. His first contribution to the conversation.

'Course not,' agreed Keeva. 'Nobody is the ma and da of Gogo. She's too old.'

'Aye,' affirmed Dylan. 'Papa Dante says that she was an old lady even when the mountains were still but mist.'

As they talked they picked up dry wood. Keeva piled the lighter sticks of kindling into Sam's arms and Dylan carried the larger logs.

They came across a circle of mushrooms under an oak tree and Keeva stopped. She pulled up the front of her skirt to form a pouch and started to pick them, brushing the soil from the roots as she collected.

Both Sam and Dylan simply stood and watched, arms full of wood. When she was finished she stood up. 'Come on, let's go back.'

She skipped ahead of them as they returned, singing softly as she did. By the time they got back to the tabor things had fallen into a semblance of order. Wood was piled for the night. Three fires were on the go. One large in the center and two separate smaller ones to each side.

Keeva's find of woodland mushrooms was greeted with applause and she curtsied after handing them over. They were then added to a huge pot of stew that was bubbling next to one of the smaller fires. Canvas water bags had been hung on some of the vardos and Sam noticed that they all seemed to be leaking.

He pointed at one of them and asked Keeva. 'Why do all of your water bottles leak? Are they broken?'

Keeva shook her head. 'It's to keep the water cold, silly,' she said.

'How does it work?'

The little girl shook her head again. 'Don't know.'

'So why am I silly then, you must also be silly.'

Dylan laughed. 'He got you there, Keeva.' He turned to talk to Sam. 'The bags leak a bit so that, when the wind blows and evaporates the water, it cools the bag down, just like sweating makes us cool. So there, Sam the man. Now you know.'

Mama started clapping her hands and calling out. 'Come on everyone. To table now.'

Everyone converged on the long trestle table set out in the middle of the encampment, except for four of the men, one at each quarter of the circle, who sat on top of the vardos, watching outward. Vigilant.

Supper consisted of stew and potatoes. The stew may have contained some chicken, Sam wasn't sure, but mainly it was vegetable. Thick, nourishing and tasty. Mugs were filled with clear cold water that tasted faintly of the canvas it was stored in. It was not an unpleasant taste.

But what held Sam's attention for the whole meal was the old lady who sat at the head of the table. She had come out of her vardo when Mama had clapped and she had walked straight to her seat at the table, aided only with her walking cane, despite the obvious fact that she was totally blind. Both eyes a blank white stare of opaque cataracts.

At the end of the meal, Sam stood up to help clear the plates and the old women pointed at him. 'Boy,' she said. Her voice clear and strong with the timber of youth. 'Come sit here, Gogo will talk to thee.'

Sam walked the length of the table and stood next to the old lady.

'Bring thy face to me,' she commanded.

Sam lent forward and she put her hands on his face. Lightly feeling.

'Aye,' she said. 'You'll be all right. You will stay with Keeva and her folk. Now, we can't be having that English name, my boy. Now you be one of us your name be Somhairle.'

'That's hard to say.'

'You're right, boy. But never you mind because the short version of Somhairle is Sam.'

'So, I'm still Sam?'

'Aye,' agreed Gogo. 'But now you are more than you were before. Now, go to Keeva and she will introduce you to your new family.'

Sam walked back down the table. Keeva greeted him with a curtsey and then put her arms around him and kissed both his cheeks. Then she stood back and gestured to a man and a lady standing next to her.

'This is my da,' she said. 'And this is my ma.'

The man was cast from the same mold as the other Pavees, tall and wiry, dark skin, black hair and beard with eyes like chips of winter sky.

He went down on one knee in front of Sam. 'Greeting and welcome, young Somhairle,' he said. 'I be Fergus. You may call me Fergus or da, whatever makes you more comfortable.' He hugged Sam and kissed him on both cheeks.

Next the lady knelt before him. She went through the same ritual of hugging and kissing on both cheeks. 'Greeting Somhaile, son,' she said. 'My name is Clodagh, but it would greatly please me if you could call me ma.'

Then all three of Sam's new family knelt on the floor and hugged him close.

And, for the first time, Sam felt safe enough to cry for the loss of his true parents.

Chapter 23

Nathaniel stared across the green rolling hills at the rows and rows of men. There must be at least four or five thousand of them, he thought to himself. Most of them were busy hauling on many long ropes. The ropes were attached to massive stone blocks that looked to be about six foot wide and at least twenty-five foot long. The Marine figured them to weigh in at around forty tons.

The blocks were being towed atop massive wooden sleighs with smooth runners carved from entire trees. In front of each runner walked teams of men with what looked like buckets of animal fat. Using ladles they were pouring the animal fat into the path of the runners. Another group of men were clearing the way of stones and impediments. The going was slow but steady.

He saw two men approaching him, striding up the hill, their white robes billowing around them as they came. One of them carried with him a stout staff and the other a bright sickle. They were quite obviously druids.

Nathaniel felt for his colt 45 but, instead, his hands discovered the haft of an axe. The weapon was a simple one. It stood around four foot high, the butterfly shaped double blades at least eighteen inches wide. The oak shaft two inches across and covered in brass studs. The handle covered in strips of wound leather.

A weapon for killing, not for show.

He glanced down to see with surprise that not only was his weapon different, so was his clothing. He was dressed entirely in steel armor. And, when he looked more closely at it, it was apparent that the armor had been fashioned out of old car parts. The Japanese Nissan symbol for their Infiniti car was emblazoned across his breastplate. The rest of the steel had been enameled in deep black.

It was then that he realized that he was dreaming and he grinned to himself.

'Bloody weird,' he mumbled under his breath.

The druids got to within a few feet of him and both of them took a knee.

'Our humble greetings to the Forever Man,' said the one.

'Through the dark hours of man's night may you protect and surround us,' the other intoned.

'Greetings, druidic dudes,' said Nathaniel. 'I know that this is just a dream but, is that Stonehenge that you're all building?'

'That is the Hooded Gate, Forever Man, methinks that it is called Stanhenge in your times. It is how we tell when and where the Life-Light will occur so that we may rekindle our magiks.'

Nathaniel slapped himself across the face. Hard. It stung. But that doesn't prove anything, he thought to himself. When you get hurt in a dream then it often does actually feel sore. He tried to wake up.

'You dream not, Fear Go Deo,' said that druid with the sickle.

'Bloody well am,' countered Nathaniel.

'Nay, Fear Go Deo, you have traveled, through time and space to see us.'

'What's Fear Go Deo?' Asked the Marine.

'Tis your name, the Forever Man. You have ever been known thus. And ever will thou be thus known.'

'Right,' said Nathaniel. 'I give up, may as well go with the flow. So, dude, why am I here?'

'You need both warning and guidance.'

'Hit me then,' said Nathaniel.

'Firstly, you must seek the other and, secondly, beware the folk that are fair and, finally, remember, when all appears lost, thine enemy of thine enemy is thine friend.'

'Woah,' said Nathaniel. 'For a start, who is the other?'

'Your time with us grows short. Remember, beware the fair folk.'

Nathaniel felt himself fading. Waking. The druid with the sickle grabbed his arm and slashed the back of the Marine's hand with the tip of the blade, twisting the sickle as he did. Almost as if he were writing something. Pain shot up his arm.

And he sat up in his bed.

The Marine chuckled to himself. It had seemed so real. The feel of the wind on his face, the smells. The pain in his hand. He picked his hand up and looked at it.

Blood ran freely down the cut and dripped onto his bed.

And, carved into the back of his hand was the symbol, an 8 on its side.

∞

Lemniscate - the sign for Infinity.

The mark of the Forever Man.

Chapter 24

Commander Ammon was exhausted. As soon as he and Seth had returned from the blue green planet, they had called for a meeting of the council and put forward their options. The decision had been made. And it had been made easily, as the alternatives were little more than a choice between go and live, or stay and die.

Now he had to prepare for the withdrawal and evacuation of close on one and a half million beings.

All told there were approximately 100 000 fair folk. 80 000 constructs, 800 000 battle Orcs, 10 000 trolls and 400 000 goblins.

Firstly Ammon had ordered mass hunting to take place. All edible animals both domesticated and wild, were killed, quartered and smoked or salt-cured. Maize meal was ground and stored in sacks, vegetables were pickled, fruits became jams and barrels of flour for bread were stocked up. This was to ensure that, when they got to their new home, they had at least six months worth of provisions.

As well as food he started stocking extra arrows by the hundreds of thousands, spears, armor, handcarts, tents, shovels, cooking pots and swords. Everything that he would need to start what would basically be a huge tent city surrounded by a stockade. He had not noticed a great number of trees in the area they were heading to so even the stockades had to be prefabricated ready to be transported through the gate.

At the same time, Ammon could not allow the hive to suspect that something untoward was happening. So, he had instituted a series of lightning strikes against the enemy. Sending his fast, mobile Orc battle groups deep into enemy territory to slash and burn. Cut supply lines. Raid camps and put tents and other structures to the torch.

The first party through the gate were to consist of a handful of fair folk officers, five thousand Orcs and five thousand goblins. Their remit was to secure the area. Once that was achieved then the rest of the nation would be fed through the gate.

He would leave a rearguard of mixed troops defending the gateway until the last possible moment and then they too, hopefully, would be brought through to their new world.

The major thing that worried Ammon was the beings of the new planet (Seth had told him that the inhabitants named it Earth, so he'd better get used to calling it such. Also, Seth had said that the beings were Humans, so that was another one to remember). Although Seth had assured him that the humans were experiencing some sort of meltdown in their civilization it was obvious from the mage's other stories of Earth's history that the humans had, at one stage, been unbelievably powerful. And without magik. A purely technological power. Actually, that had not been strictly true. As Ammon had pointed out to Seth, the very gateway itself was going to open in a circle of Light stones or, standing stones. And that proved that magik had, at least at some stage in the extremely distant past, been well used. But again Seth had assured him; the magik had long since died out. There was little to worry about. They would be the superior beings.

As well as their lack of magik, Seth had noted that they were extremely susceptible to the Fair-Folk's glamouring skills. This was the talent that the Fair-Folk had since birth. A way of letting people see what they wanted to see when looking at them. It was an ancient survival technique that they had, of late, had little use for but, when actually physically entering a new realm or planet it would serve them well.

Seth had conducted many experiments in his Earthly travels and had concluded that, with a small amount of concentration, the human beings could be persuaded to see the Fair-Folk as tall, well muscled, handsome and blond versions of themselves. However, when they first saw the Orcs, Goblins and Trolls they would see true. The magikal-biological constructs that the Fair Folk bred would also be seen as their true selves; however, they were, on appearance, similar to human children. Small, smooth skinned, large eyes, a fuzzy crop of hair on their heads. The only major difference being that they were possessed of two fully adult sets of genitalia. After all, they had been designed not only to fetch and carry but also to provide entertainment for the soldiers after battle.

Ammon had also been toying with a few ideas. He had not broached the subject with Seth or any other members of the council yet. But he was convinced that, due to the humans ease at being glamoured, they might find that there would be no need to create any new constructs. It may be that they could simply glamour the humans into doing their will, and doing so gratefully.

However, those thoughts were for later. For now he had a mountain of administrative work and then he needed some rest. A full night's sleep would be perfect but a couple of hours would suffice.

He drew his cloak closer around his shoulders to ward off the chill and set to his work.

Chapter 25

Axel had gotten the villagers to build fires. Many fires. They had also put together a couple of hundred torches. The torches were as rudimentary as one could imagine. A three-foot length of wood, the end wrapped in bandages torn from sheets until it looked like a giant Q-tip. These had been soaked in cooking oil and then distributed amongst the people.

The officers had also helped make up around one hundred Molotov cocktails. There wasn't enough time to get very fancy about them so they were simply a mixture of gasoline and diesel fuel in a glass bottle with a rag stuffed into the neck. Axel figured that these would be good both as defense and as illumination.

Axel had also gathered all of the villagers together and talked to them. He had advised that the women and children were retired to the village church with five armed men and when, or if, the day was lost, they were to attempt to make a run for it.

Patrick walked up to Axel who was standing on the wall, looking out across the fields. He carried with him an implausibly expensive bottle of red wine from Axel's father's cellar, and two cut crystal glasses. In his shirt pocket he had stuffed a few cigars.

He poured wine into the glasses and held one out to his friend. Axel took it.

'Cheers.'

Patrick toasted back. 'Cheers. Health, wealth and all that crap.' He held the glass up to the setting sun. The light caught the crystal and spread a rainbow over his unshaven face that matched the ever-present multicolor coruscation in the sky. A Kandinsky painting. Or perhaps an early Mondrian. 'I always though that I'd get mine in Afghanistan,' Patrick continued. 'Or maybe some toilet in Africa. Definitely did not expect rural, bloody England. What about you?'

Axel shrugged. 'Thought that I'd survive. Maybe make Major then retire, take over the family business. Get married, have a bunch of rug-rats. Get gout, have a stroke, premature baldness. Normal. Just normal.'

Patrick laughed. 'Christ, kill me now. Really? Is that how you saw your future?'

Axel nodded. 'Ordinary, you know. No EMP strikes or solar flares. No fighting hoards of psychotic criminals in a village in the middle of an English county. Definitely no end-of-the-world scenarios. Tea with the vicar, village cricket, Pimms and cucumber bloody sandwiches. Where's Dom?'

Patrick grinned. 'With that fat blonde bird from the post office.'

'Who, Sweaty-Betty?'

'That's the one. He figured that he deserved a last shag and she was the only one whom he reckoned was a definite.'

'Well,' said Axel. 'He's correct there.'

Patrick pulled out two cigars and bit the ends off them. Flicked his Zippo and got one going, handed it to Axel and then worked on his own.

The two of them stood in compatible silence for a while as the sun sank slowly behind the trees.

'I reckon they'll come around ten o'clock,' said Axel. 'Maybe later. But not earlier. And they'll come slowly, clear a path, chuck ladders against the walls. Rely on the dark to shield them.'

'So what do we do?' Asked Patrick.

'We wait. Keep our eyes skinned. Think we see something, anything, we throw a Molotov at the movement and see what happens.'

After a few more minutes Axel left Patrick at the wall and went for a walk around the village. He stopped wherever he saw people and chatted. Lifting spirits, cracking jokes, giving advice. The vicar was holding a service in the village square. A short and simple one.

'When you go out to war against your enemies,' said the vicar. 'And you see horses and chariots and an army larger than your own, you shall not be afraid of them, for the Lord your God is with you. And when you draw near to the battle, the priest shall come forward and speak to the people and shall say to them, Hear, O Israel, today you are drawing near for battle against your enemies: let not your heart faint. Do not fear or panic or be in dread of them, for the Lord your God is he who goes with you to fight for you against your enemies.'

'Hallelujah, father,' whispered Axel.

Someone touched Axel on the shoulder and he spun around quickly. His nerves on edge.

'Whoa, boy.'

It was Dom, rifle in hand and ridiculous broadsword strapped across his back.

'Surveying the troops?' Asked Dom.

'Yah,' agreed Axel. 'Poor bastards. They don't deserve this.'

'And we do?'

'It's different. Butcher, baker and candlestick maker. Not soldier.'

'What can I say?' Asked Dom. 'Sometimes life gives you lemons and there's bugger all that you can do about it. Sometimes being a soldier simply sucks the big one. Remember what Colonel Biggums used to say?'

Both of the young men spoke together; 'Please don't tell my mum that I'm a soldier, she thinks that I play the piano in a whorehouse.'

Axel laughed. Genuine happy laughter.

'We'd better take up our positions. Won't be long now.' He turned to face the vicar and shouted. 'Father. Positions please.'

All around became a roil of movement. People running to the walls, lighting torches, saying last second prayers.

And Axel was correct. They didn't have to wait long. Although the moon was less than half full it was a cloudless night and, with the extra aurora, one could pick out movement at about thirty yards. Axel lit up a Molotov and heaved it at the area that he suspected. The flaming bottle arced through the air and exploded on the ground, flaring up in a burst of yellow flame. The firelight clearly picked out a group of men crawling along the ground, dragging a ladder behind them. The villagers on

Axel's wall opened up with their shotguns, spraying the area with buckshot. Then the flame went out and the night seemed even darker than before.

Axel heard the crump of exploding bottles coming from the other walls as similar scenarios unfolded.

It was the beginning of a long night.

The next two hours carried on in the same way. The thump of Molotovs exploding accompanied by short smatterings of small arms fire.

And then the intensity of firing increased at Patrick's wall. Axel glanced over to see Molotovs sailing in from the other side of the wall. Six, seven, eight of them. One struck a villager in the chest and he went up like a Guy. A stuffed straw man except for the screaming and rolling about. Other villagers threw buckets of water on him and the fire sizzled to a steaming halt but the screaming continued.

He saw a ladder thump against the top of the wooden fence. Patrick ran along the walkway and kicked the ladder off, leaning over and firing his shotgun into the faces of the people below. People fired back and Axel saw Patrick take a hit, his hair flicking up as buckshot pellets struck him. But although blood poured down from his scalp he appeared to be okay with the injury.

And then there were people at Axel's wall. Running in hard, twenty or thirty of them appearing out of the dark. Their clothes and faces blackened with mud. Carrying ladders. Maybe seven or eight sets of them. Axel aimed his Webley and started to fire. The old handgun booming like a cannon. Next to him shotguns cracked and Molotovs fluttered through the air, bursting in billows of flames.

The ladders thudded up against the fence. Axel reloaded and walked to the top of the first ladder, kicking it sideways so that it slid off the wall, taking another one with it. People came boiling over the top of the next ladder and Axel shot them as they came, the Webley bucking in his hand like a live animal. Two other male villagers were using their makeshift spears, jabbing at the faces of the criminals as they climbed the ladders. There was a volley of fire from the bottom of the fence and both of the spear-wielding villagers went down in a welter of blood. Axel reloaded again, fired, reloaded. The old pistol red-hot. Every time he touched it, his skin would blister and slough off. After the seventh reload, the rounds started to cook off in the barrel. The captain dropped the revolver to the ground, its usefulness over.

He swung the pump action shotgun off its sling over his shoulder and started to fire at the attackers. Rapidly, pumping the action as fast as he could.

And then the fence was clear. They had beaten the attackers back.

Axel turned to survey Patrick's wall only to be greeted by a scene of total disaster. Not only had the enemy breached the defenses, they had actually smashed down a portion of the fence and were pouring in.

But even worse than that, the vicar's fence had also gone and Axel could see that the church was surrounded, already burning strongly as a group of the prisoners threw Molotov after Molotov at it. The roaring of the flames almost drowning out the screams of the women and children trapped inside.

Axel grabbed a spear and reloaded the shotgun as he ran to assist, anger and hatred swamping his other emotions in a blind fury. He gestured at five other villagers. 'With me,' he shouted. 'The rest of you stay on this wall.'

As soon as he had reloaded he started firing from the hip, taking out two men by the time he got to the mêlée. And then it was hand-to-hand. He slashed at man's throat and the knife on the broomstick cut deep. Blood sprayed in an arc and he went down. Axel spun and smashed the butt of his makeshift spear into another attacker's temple, then he raised it high and stabbed down into his clavicle, plunging the blade deep, turning and withdrawing.

More of the Belmarsh boys were pouring in through the gap, forcing the villagers back, step by bloody step.

Patrick had lost his rifle and now also wielded a spear, fighting like a demon. A combination of MMA and animal fury. He glanced across at Axel and laughed. The bastard was enjoying himself. Doing what he had been trained to do. He pivoted and struck again, slashing and parrying. And then a massive thug came at him, wielding his empty shotgun like a baseball bat. Patrick raised his spear to block the blow but it was to no avail, the weapon merely shattered the cheap wooden handle and smashed into Patrick's temple. He went down like a stone and another three prisoners piled in. Kicking and stabbing him on the ground.

Axel shouted his friend's name and fought desperately to get to him but it was too late, Patrick's body lay broken on the ground, limbs twisted and bleeding, his life draining out of him into the English sod.

Then Axel heard a scream, a cross between a war cry and a shriek of agony as Dom came sprinting around the corner, brandishing his ridiculously huge broadsword. He smashed into the group that had just taken Patrick's life swinging the sword and screaming. The four attackers went down in a welter of blood and body parts. This didn't even slow the young man down as he waded forward, hacking and slashing. All around him torches had fallen to the floor and fires were spreading. The night aglow as the flames jumped from building to building. Someone ran up behind Dom and, before Axel could shout a warning, placed his shotgun against the back of his head and pulled the trigger. The young captain went down in a cloud of blood and brains.

Axel glanced around him. There were over a hundred Belmarsh boys in the perimeter now and, however hard he looked, there seemed to be no villagers left standing.

And, unhurriedly, a ring formed around him. He held his makeshift spear at port turning slowly, trying to keep as many people in his line of vision as possible. Eventually a large man stepped into the circle. He stared at Axel for a while and then smiled and raised his shotgun to his shoulder. 'You lost,' he said.

Axel lunged forward with his spear but it was too late.

The man pulled the trigger and the compacted shotgun pellets hit Axel in the side of his head, tearing out his eye and ripping at his flesh and skull.

The captain fell to his knees and toppled over.

The battle for the village of Judge's Cross was over.

Chapter 26

Doctor Janice Burt had been driving on the A1 highway heading back to Lester House private hospital to check on her patients when the pulse first hit. Initially she had thought that her car had stalled and tried to restart it. Secondly she noticed the lack of noise. An eerie silence in the midst of thousands of cars. She opened her car door and stepped out into the new world.

She knew nothing about EMP strikes, nor solar flares nor gamma rays. But she knew that something terrible had happened. Something both life changing and utterly beyond her control.

The next thing she noticed was the uncanny light in the skies. An oily spread of rainbow color. And, as she stared up at it she saw a distant airplane tumble from the sky. A huge passenger craft. Again, with an eerie lack of sound. It simply fell, spinning and diving until it hit the ground and exploded. Many seconds later the crump of the explosion struck her eardrums. A muted thud, like a child's book hitting the floor.

By now everyone had gotten out of their vehicles and were all asking the same questions. Stupid, unanswerable questions. Janice did not take part in the general panic. She grabbed her coat, her map book, a bottle of water and her doctors bag and started to walk.

She had decided to walk to her parents' home in Tempsford. She knew that it was far. Days away on foot. But her parents were frail, they would need help, and so that was where she would head for.

Janice walked for an hour, heading straight up the A1 motorway. At times she walked in a group of people all heading the same way, at other times she walked through stationary groups of people and, sometimes, for very short periods, she was almost alone. Everyone had theories on what was happening. They ranged from some sort of national power outage to alien invasion and even the second coming of Christ. Janice had no idea but she was sure of one thing. Whatever had caused it, it was a catastrophic event.

The fact that puzzled her the most, was that the majority of people were doing nothing. They simply sat in, or next to, their motor vehicles and waited. Waiting for the authorities to do something. The Automobile Association, the police, the army. Someone. But always, someone else.

She stopped walking for a while, took a sip of water and looked, once again, at the swirling mass of color that ebbed and flowed across the skies.

'Aurora Borealis,' said a voice at her shoulder.

She flinched in shock.

'I'm sorry. Didn't mean to startle you. Ronald Digby, professor emeritus, St. Johns college, Oxford.'

She turned to see and old gentleman. Tweed jacket, hat, horn-rimmed glasses. A pipe. As if someone had packaged together a professor using every known cliché in the book.

'No. Not a problem,' said Janice. 'Lost in my own thoughts.' She held out her hand. 'Doctor Janice Burt.' They shook hands. 'Sorry. What did you say?'

'Aurora Borealis. Northern lights. Well, strictly speaking, not the Northern lights but a very similar event. Basically, the result of collisions between gaseous particles in the Earth's atmosphere with charged particles released from the sun's atmosphere. Massive solar activity on an unprecedented scale. In Medieval times they were said to be the harbingers of war and famine.'

'Is that why nothing is working?' Asked Janice.

'Indubitably,' answered the older man. 'The solar activity has caused some sort of electromagnetic pulse that has fried all of our electrical systems.'

'How long before it all starts to work again?'

Professor Digby took off his glasses, cleaned them on the front of his jacket, replaced them. 'Never, my girl,' he answered.

'What do you mean?'

Professor Digby smiled. A wan expression, more of scholarly interest than of actual humor. 'I mean, my dear girl, that we are all well and truly rogered. Up the proverbial without a paddle. Take a good look around you and remember it, for this is the end of civilization as we know it.' He took out a bag of tobacco and started to pack his pipe.

'Are you serious?' Insisted Janice.

'Oh yes,' said the old man. 'As a heart attack, my dear girl. As a heart attack.'

Janice literally reeled back, her face shroud-white. 'I have to go,' she said. 'My parents.'

Professor Digby puffed on his pipe, bringing the tobacco to life. 'On your way, my girl,' he said. 'Be careful. If I were you I would stay off the beaten track as much as possible. Remember, my dear; Break the skin of civilization and beneath you will find the ape, roaring and red-handed. I would give society another day or so before she starts to crack. And once it's gone, dear girl, well then, all the king's horses and all the king's men shall not be able to put her back together again.' He puffed at his pipe and stared up at the sky, alone in his thoughts.

Janice continued down the road, her initial sense of adventure now one of distress and unease. After another couple of miles she took the professor's advice and left the highway, heading down a more rural road that ran roughly parallel.

The weather was mild but, as the sun began to sink low, the temperature started to drop rather dramatically. This did not bother Janice unduly as she was carrying her thick coat with her.

The houses were large but not far from the road. Four bedrooms, garage, open gates. She could see the flicker of candlelight in many of them. In some, the harsher white light of gas lamps. She had not thought this far when she had started walking and decided to throw herself on the mercy of strangers. Even the nutty old professor had said that humanity would remain intact for the next twenty-four hours. She laughed softly to herself as she recalled his conversation. At best he had been overreacting and, at worst, scare mongering.

She chose a house at random and walked down the short driveway to the front door, her shoes crunching on the gravel as she did. Her tentative knock brought the sound of footsteps and the door opened to reveal a late-middle-aged man, balding, thick glasses and tartan sweater. In his hand a candle in a silver-plated candlestick holder.

'I'm so sorry,' said Janice. 'My car stopped on the motorway and…'

The man smiled at her. 'Come in, dear. Come in. We already have a couple here. Stranded like you.'

Janice walked in and he closed the door behind her.

He stuck out his hand. 'Geoffrey. Geoffrey Chancellor. Call me Geoff.'

Janice shook it. 'Janice. Doctor Janice Burt.'

'Ooh,' he said. 'A doctor. Very impressive. Now,' he continued. 'Follow me, I'm sure you'd like a sit down and a nice cup of tea.'

She followed the man through to his sitting room and he introduced her all round. Then he went to the kitchen to make tea. Janice assumed that he must have some sort of gas camping stove.

There were three other people in the room; Gail Chancellor and another younger couple Tom Ashford and Mary Jobe. After a round of handshaking, Geoff reappeared with a mug of tea and a jar of sugar.

'Here you go, love. Sorry, no milk. Ran out this morning and couldn't get to the shops.'

Janice spooned some sugar into the mug, stirred briefly and took it from her host.

'Now,' continued Geoff. 'You're welcome to stay the night, Janice. As I told Tom and Mary, I'm sure that the power will be back on by tomorrow morning.'

'Why?' Asked Janice.

Geoff did a slight double take. 'I'm sorry, dear. Why what?'

'Why do you think that the power will be on by tomorrow?'

'Well,' chipped in Gail. 'The people will put it back on. Fix it, you know.'

'Which people?'

Gail looked flustered. 'The people that fix it. The people in charge.'

'I don't mean to be obtuse or such,' said Janice. 'But how will they fix our cars?' She held up her wristwatch, the hands stilled at 6.11 pm, the moment of the pulse. 'Our watches,' continued Janice. 'The cell phone network. The trains. The airplanes.'

Nobody said anything for a while. A tear rolled down Gail Chancellor's cheek. A tiny candle-lit jewel.

'They'll fix it,' she whispered.

Geoff stood up. 'Come on,' he said. His voice bursting with forced bonhomie. 'Let's make up the beds. An early night and things will all seem much better in the morning.'

***

Janice slept surprisingly well, waking at just before six the next morning.

Contrary to what Geoff had said, things did not seem better in the morning. In fact, things seemed a lot worse.

He was already awake when Janice went through to the sitting room and he glanced up as she entered.

'Good morning,' she greeted.

He nodded at her. Then he spoke. 'I'm sorry, Janice. Can't offer tea. There's no water coming out of the taps. Bit low on food as well, actually. I think that I'd better take a walk to the local shops. Get some essentials in.'

Janice nodded her agreement. 'Don't worry about me, Geoff. I need to be on my way.'

Geoff didn't react. Merely sat with his

hands between his knees. Staring vacantly at the floor.

Janice went back to her bedroom and picked up her coat and doctors bag. Just before she left, she took her empty water bottle and went through to the bathroom. She checked the taps but Geoff was right. No water. So she carefully lifted the top of the toilet cistern. Full. She placed the bottle under the water, filled it, put the top back on and slid it into her bag.

She left via the front door, leaving without saying goodbye. Once again the sky was filled with the oily rainbow of light that had been so prevalent the day before and, once again, she was struck by the fundamental silence of the world around her. No cars, airplanes, trains, radios or TV's. The aural detritus of modern man reduced to nature's backing track. Wind and birdsong. Breath and heartbeat.

She walked all morning, taking a sip from her bottle every now and then. She came across small groups of people who, on the whole, simply ignored her. All caught up in their own fear and trepidation.

Late morning she came to a small group of shops. A mini strip mall. It was here that she saw professor Digby's theory of the breaking of civilization at first hand. The convenience store, a tiny Mom and Pop of the type usually filled with fresh bread and milk and boxes of chocolate and biscuits so old that the boxes were sun-faded into mere facsimiles of their original. Cheap plastic children's toys, tins of no-name chilli con carne, overpriced cans of soda and budget birthday cards sold at upscale prices.

But the shop contained none of these things. No toys, no soda…nothing. The front windows had been smashed and the shop completely stripped. Sitting on the pavement outside was an old man, early seventies. He held a cloth to his head. It was red with blood, as was the side of his face.

Janice knelt down beside him.

'Are you all right?' She asked.

He raised his head to look at her. His eyes unfocused. 'They took it,' he said. 'I knew them all. This morning when I opened up they all just poured in, snatching stuff from the shelves. Panic. Some paid. Some didn't. I tried to stop them and they hit me. Mister Johnson. Patrick the plumber. Even Mister Soames from the local school. Like animals. They pushed me down and kicked me.'

Janice probed at the wound on his forehead. It was deep. Through to the bone. She opened her bag and took out some bandages and a tube of Dermabond. The old man said nothing as she cleaned the wound, closed it with the Dermabond glue and wrapped a bandage around his head.

'Thank you,' he said when she had finished. 'You're very kind.'

Janice patted his hand and stood up. 'I have to go,' she said. 'I'm heading for my parents. Take care.'

'You too, doctor,' he said. 'And be careful. The lunatics have taken over the asylum.'

That evening, Janice found herself in the tiny village of Stuckham. Two roads of thatch cottages, a plant nursery and an antiques store. She picked one of the smaller cottages that had candlelight flickering in the window and knocked on the door.

She could hear people inside walking around and whispered voices. Eventually the door peeked open.

'Hello,' she greeted.

'Go away.' A male voice. Late middle age. Nervous.

'Please,' continued Janice. 'I mean no harm. I'm a doctor and I'm on my way to see my parents. I was simply looking for a place to spend the night. A piece of floor out of the elements.'

There was a terse whispered conversation behind the door. Then the man spoke again

'You can sleep in the shed around the side. Here,' a hand passed a blanket through the opening. 'Sorry. Best we can do.' The door slammed shut and Janice heard the bolt being drawn across and the sound of a table or similar piece of furniture pulled in front of it as well.

Janice walked around the side of the cottage and found the garden shed. It was small but tidy. A lawnmower, sacks of grass seed. Old tins of paint. She laid the sacks out to form a bed, rolled up in the blanket and lay down.

Sleep came in fits and starts accompanied by nightmares of such vividness that at times she was unsure of where reality ended and nightmare began. Eventually she realized that the mere fact of sleeping did not define the nightmare. The nightmare had become defined by reality. Life, as she knew it, was fundamentally over. The new dark ages had begun and reality was now the nightmare.

She arose as soon as it was light enough to see. She filled her water bottle from the rainwater butt next to the house. She took the blanket with her. It was her third day without food and she was starting to feel weak.

But she had to get to her parents, so she put one foot in front of the other and repeated.

The days wore on.

Chapter 27

He felt pain. And more than pain. It was as though the flesh had been scoured from his face and then doused in gasoline. But he welcomed it. Reveled in it. Because it meant that he was alive.

Slowly, he rose to his knees and peered around. His vision was…odd. He could see, but not in the same way. He felt the right side of his face. Pain flared, burning across his head. Sticky. He felt further, ignoring the agony. Wet flesh. No eye.

'Damn,' he mumbled to himself. 'bloody lost an eye.'

The world swung around him as he stood up. His remaining vision exploded into a light show of star-bursts and sparklers.

He scanned his surrounds. Fire. Smoke. The village was burning. Dead bodies lay scattered with careless hand. All male. No females. Some had died alone. Others in couples or groups. Sprawled all over each other. Comradeship in death. He looked for a weapon. Couldn't see one so he wandered through the burning village, unarmed. Seeking out life.

In the village square he found the women, and girls. All naked. All dead. Covered in blood. Raped. All ages. Hatred washed over him like a tsunami. So strong that it pushed aside his pain, leaving only a burning desire for revenge. For vengeance.

But first he had to find water, and food. And then weapons. So, moving slowly so as to minimize the waves of pain, Axel walked through the village, seeking supplies, his hatred driving him like a small fissionable reactor.

Chapter 28

Nathaniel sat at the table in his room and attempted to roll a cigarette with his new homemade ingredients. He had dried some Hazel leaves and some mint, chopped it up and was now rolling it in a scrap of paper.

He stared at his finished product with some trepidation. It looked right but smelt odd. The Zippo was flicked into flame. Applied. He dragged.

When the Professor entered his room, some five minutes later, he was still coughing.

'Goodness me,' exclaimed the Prof. 'Smells like a bonfire in here. What are you burning?'

Nathaniel held up the offending tube of ersatz tobacco. 'Trying to make cigarettes. Hazel and mint.'

The Prof laughed. 'Smells disgusting. Anyhow,' he continued. 'On a more serious subject. It appears that we have lost two of the scholars.'

'What do you mean, lost?'

'Well, I assume that they left on their own accord. Brother and sister. Tom and Louise. Their parents lived fairly close by. Twenty miles or so. I think that they may have gone to find them.'

'Well good luck to them,' said Nathaniel.

'They're only fifteen and sixteen years old, master sergeant.'

The Marine sighed. 'Suppose that you want me to go after them?'

'If you could,' agreed the Prof.

'Fine. Have you got a map of the surrounds showing where the parents live? I'll go alone. I'll tool up just in case, one never knows what uglies are out there. Bring me a couple of candles as well, please Prof.'

While Nathaniel kitted up the Professor went to fetch a map. He returned and handed over the candles, then he showed Nathaniel the route that the teenagers would most likely have taken.

'When did they go?' Asked Nathaniel.

'They were at breakfast,' said the Prof. 'But no one saw them at lunch. That's when the others told me. We checked their rooms and they weren't there. Plus some clothes, a haversack, water bottles were missing.'

'So. Maybe four hours. Maybe as much as six. I'll catch them.' He hitched the strap for his M249M22 machine gun over his shoulder. He had the one belt of 200 rounds, leaving the rest of the ammo on the bed. He also holstered his 45 and two extra magazines. He wore no body armor.

He left via the front gate, looked at the map, got his bearings and jogged off. A fast, loping run that he could continue all day if he had to.

For the first hour he ran down the only road. A winding, one lane country track with trees so thick that their overhanging branches formed a leaf covered passageway. Every now and then he would come across a gate. He would always stop and check if there was anything in the field. Cows, horses, sheep, people. But he saw nothing.

During the second hour he came across a sheep lying next to the road. Its carcass bloated. Missing legs. Throat cut. It had been inexpertly butchered by someone who carried away what they could and had left the rest.

The Marine cast around for spoor. Two people. One older, heavier. The other young. Small. Father and child? Mother and daughter? Nathaniel stood up and started to run once again.

He came to a crossroads and, after consulting the map, turned left. After a mile, a T-junction. Consult map. Turn left again. Nathaniel kept moving fast, worried as the light bled from the afternoon and the sky began to bruise with the coming of evening.

He came across a car. Abandoned, one door open. He checked for anything worthwhile but it was empty.

Finally he came to a small hamlet, at the bottom of a dip, surrounded by trees. Perhaps seven houses. Small cottages and one large Tudor mansion. A little way past the hamlet sat a small church or chapel. It was only a single story high. Small buttresses stood out from the walls and a row of arched windows ran down its length. It looked like a 17th century flat-pack church. Graceless and ugly. A stone toad squatting in the English countryside, dark and forbidding in the lowering light.

Nathaniel knocked on the doors of the cottages, calling out. All of the doors were locked but no one answered. He looked at the church and thought that there just might be a light on inside. A single candle, perhaps. He walked towards the squat stone building, a feeling of trepidation filling him for no real reason apart from the odd appearance of the small ugly building.

It was only when he got close to the narthex of the building, a wooden picket fence with a rough wooden roof, that his unease grew into full concern. The intricate wooden cross that graced the entrance to the church had been ripped off and then re-nailed back up. But this time it was upside down. The Marine did not need to get any closer to see what the dark, almost black, fluid was that covered it. He could smell the iron smell of blood from where he stood.

He moved forward with stealth. Pushed the door open just enough to squeeze through.

There were maybe twelve or fifteen people in the church. Lit by six candles. Dull, orange guttering light. The people were dressed in robes of dark material. And, laid out on the floor of the chancel, in front of the alter, were two naked bodies. Despite the dull lighting Nathaniel recognized them instantly as Tom and Louise. Standing over them was another man, also dressed in a hooded robe. He held a book in one hand and a long silver blade in the other. The edge of the blade was covered in blood and Nathaniel could see that an upside down crucifix had been cut into both of the teenager's chests, the stipes running between their breasts and the patibulum slashed across their lower abdomen. The cuts weren't as deep as to need stitches but they were deep enough to allow the blood to flow freely from them. It was their blood that had been used to desecrate the cross outside.

Tom was staring at the hooded figure with undisguised hatred. Louise was whimpering, her eyes clenched tightly shut.

The hooded man was chanting something in Latin.

'Dominus malum, accipe nos.'

Nathaniel's limited knowledge of Latin was based more on street Italian than the classics but as far as he could work out this meant something like, Dark Lord take us now. The Marine slowly raised his weapon to point at the dark priest, his movement a picture of stealth.

Then the dark priest put down the book, pulled his robes aside and started to urinate on the two bound bodies.

'No way,' shouted the Marine as he depressed the trigger to the SAW. Eight high velocity rounds smashed into the dark priest in under one second, ripping into his torso, lifting him up and throwing him bodily back into the nave, some ten feet away.

The noise of the machine gun in the enclosed stone room was beyond deafening and most of the worshippers simply fell to the floor in shock. Two of them, however, reacted with staggering speed, turning and running at the Marine. But, as fast as they thought they were, to Nathaniel's super-quick reflexes it was as if he were watching someone running at him through knee high mud. He let them get within six feet of him and then ripped off two short bursts. Five rounds each that literally tore them in half.

Then he shouted in his loudest parade ground voice.

'Listen up, crazies. Move to the right hand side of the church. Do it now or I will open fire on you.'

The hooded congregation shuffled to do his bidding, the noise and blood and the violent butchery having subdued any feelings of retaliation.

Nathaniel rushed to the two teenagers, picked up the sacrificial knife and quickly cut Tom's bonds. Then he handed the boy the knife.

'Cut your sister free,' commanded the Marine. Tom nodded, his eyes wide with shock but his movements still steady.

Nathaniel grasped his shoulder and squeezed. 'Good boy, well done.' Then the Marine chose one of the worshippers at random.

'Hey, you. Halfwit, where are their clothes?'

The worshipper said nothing. Nathaniel stepped forward, flicked the man's hood back and hit him in the face with the butt of the machine gun. He went over backwards in a welter of blood, his nose shattered and shifted to the right hand side of his face. He was unconscious before he hit the floor. Nathaniel moved to the next worshipper.

'Clothes,' he said.

They pointed at the alter. 'Behind there.'

'Fetch them,' commanded the Marine.

The man scampered over and pulled a pile of clothes from behind the altar.

'Give them to the boy.'

He handed them to Tom who sorted quickly through them, picking out his sister's underwear, jeans, t-shirt and sneakers that he gave to her. Only then did he dress himself.

Nathaniel beckoned for the two teenagers to join him.

'You guys okay?' He asked.

They both nodded.

'The bastard pissed on us,' said Tom, his voice shaking with anger.

'Yep,' agreed Nathaniel. 'But now his pissing days are long gone.' He took Louise by then shoulder. 'Are you all right? No…umm…'

Louise smiled, a slight movement of the lips. 'They didn't rape me or anything,' she said. 'Apparently that was the lord Satan's job.'

The Marine shook his head. 'Crazy animals.'

'How dare you?' Shouted one of the congregation. 'How dare you label us as crazy?

We are the Order of Nine Angels and our moment has come. No longer shall we skulk in the darkness, avoiding the unbelievers. Nay, we shall stride forth and conquer. Do you not see? The Dark Lord has brought about the new Dark Age. He has painted the sky with his colors and only those who worship him and love him shall survive. Through human sacrifice and foul deeds shall we praise his name. *Dominus malum, accipe nos.*'

The rest of the congregation joined in with the chant, their heads rocking rhythmically, eyes staring glassily forward.

'Dominus malum, accipe nos. Dominus malum, accipe nos.'

Nathaniel pulled out his Colt and handed it to Tom, slipping the safety off as he did so. 'Here, be careful, the safety is off. You point it, hold tight, pull the trigger. Anything in the way dies. Simple. Get it?'

Tom nodded.

'Good boy. Go outside with your sister and wait for me.'

The two teenagers ran from the building, eager to escape from the awful darkness and the stench of death.

By now the congregation had worked itself up into an ardor of religious ecstasy. Some were weeping openly, others were rending their hair, literally tearing it out in clumps while still others were biting their own tongues, blood flowing freely from their mouths. And then, all at once, they charged the Marine.

From outside the desecrated church the two teenagers heard the SAW open up. The sound muted by the thick stone walls. Like a gigantic typewriter typing at an incredible speed. Or the sound of a cloth being torn magnified in volume a million times.

The door swung open. Tom raised the Colt but it was only the Marine. He stood in silence for a while, the only sound the plinking of the machine gun as it cooled down in the fresh night air. Eventually he spoke.

'Now those people were what we like to call, howling at the moon crazy.'

'Did you kill them all?' Asked Louise, her voice quiet. Horror etched into her expression.

Nathaniel nodded.

'Good,' she said. 'They were evil. They deserved to die.'

'Amen and hallelujah to that,' agreed Nathaniel. 'Now, let's go through these houses, see what we can find. Then we clean you guys up, sort out your wounds and get a good night sleep. Don't worry, I'll stay awake, make sure that you're safe. Then, tomorrow we go and find you parents. Deal?'

The two teenagers smiled. 'Deal,' they said together.

When they entered the first cottage Nathaniel took the two candles that the Prof had given him and lit them, passing one to Louise and one to Tom. The cottage revealed nothing of note, the second one, however, must have had a husband and wife of almost identical size to the two teenagers. They each chose a selection of fresh clothes. Then Nathaniel took a bucket and went to the rainwater butt. After a few trips he had shallow filled a bath.

Louise washed first, cleaning the blood and sweat and urine off herself, then she wrapped up in a towel. Tom followed suit. Then the two of them went into the sitting room.

'Right,' said the Marine to Louise. 'I'm going to have to take a look at your wound. You'll have to take your towel off and cover up with your hands.'

The Marine had taken out his medical kit and selected some bandages, a tube of antibiotic cream, a packet of quick-clot, a bottle of povidone-iodine solution and adhesive tape.

Louise lay back on the sofa and dropped her towel to her hips, covering herself from just below her navel. She didn't bother to place her hands over her breasts. Her cut was still oozing blood, particularly between her breasts where the incision was deeper.

'This is going to sting a bit,' Nathaniel warned as he tore off a square of sterile bandage and soaked it with the iodine solution. He used it to swab the wound clean, working firmly but efficiently. Tears sprang to Louise's eyes but she didn't flinch. Then Nathaniel sprinkled some quick-clot over the wound and the bleeding stopped immediately. Finally he ran a length of sterile bandage down each of the cuts and stuck it on using the adhesive tape.

While he did the same to Tom, his sister dressed herself. And Tom followed.

'Well done, guys,' said Nathaniel. 'I'm proud of you. Tom, keep hold of the 45. Bring the candles. Let's check out the rest of the houses.'

The other four cottages were similarly uninteresting and it was only when they entered the Tudor mansion that things started to look up.

The malevolent occupiers of the hamlet had obviously pooled their recourses and moved them to the main house for safekeeping. It was their sick rite at the church that had drawn them all away, leaving no one to guard the hoard. The entrance hall was piled high with cases of tinned food, boxes of medical goods, sacks of dry goods, bottles of water and, even more importantly, racks of shotguns with boxes of ammunition.

'Well damn me sideways,' said Nathaniel. Louise giggled at his profanity. 'Man,' he continued. 'We'd need a five ton truck to shift all of this. Don't know how we're going to do it but we have to get it back to the abbey. Come on, guys, let's check the rest of the place out.'

The sitting room had a huge pile of wood set against the one wall, ready for cold weather and cooking in the hearth. There were also a few boxes of large church candles. In the dining room, heaps of blankets, heavy weather coats, boots, gloves and other items of clothing and more candles. The house was a treasure trove. Nathaniel was rooting through the boxes when he heard something. He stopped and listened.

'You guys hear that?' He asked.

'It's coming from there,' said Louise, pointing at a door in the dining room. Nathaniel went over and put his ear to the wood. Now he could clearly hear someone. A male voice. Singing, deep and melodious. Then the singing stopped to be replaced by the same voice swearing at the top of his lungs, the fact that they could hardly hear, testament to the thickness of the door.

'He gestured to the two teenagers. 'Stand back,' and he opened the door. 'Hey,' he shouted. 'Who's there?'

A bottle came whipping out of the darkness and shattered behind the Marine. A blood colored chrysanthemum of red wine splashed across the wall. Nathaniel took a few quick steps back into the room.

And then someone came running up the stairs. A barrel of a man. Perhaps five feet ten high by similar dimensions in width. Most likely weighing in at over three hundred pounds. He was wearing a black cassock and, on his feet, a pair of steel capped work boots.

'Ya feckin bastard,' he yelled as he ran straight into the Marine. It was like he had run into a wall and the look of surprise on his face was almost comical, had he not been so angry. He staggered about for a second or so and then sat down with a thump. Flat on his buttocks with his legs out straight in front of him. A huge child at play.

He shook his head and looked at the Marine. 'And who da feck are youse?' He demanded.

'Master gunnery sergeant Nathaniel Hogan, United Sates Marine Corp. And you?'

'I be father Phelim O'Hara. I tort dat you wus one of does devil worshippin bastards.

Dat's why I tru a bottle at yez,' said the man, his Irish accent so broad as to need serious concentration to follow what he was saying.

'Not a problem,' said Nathaniel.

The priest stood up. 'Tell me, young Marine soldier, how comes yez didna fall doon when I charged yez?'

'I make a habit of not falling down, Father.'

'Aye, be dat as it may, when Father Phelim O'Hara runs into someone dey falls down. Always dey falls down.'

'Well, you can't say that any more now, Father, can you?'

The priest shook his head sadly. 'Nay and nay again, to be sure. Still, I won't mention it ta any and I be sure dat you won't nieder. So den tell me, where are does Satan worshipping pig feckers?'

There was a pause before Nathaniel answered. 'I killed them, Father.'

O'Hara rubbed his hands together. 'Well done, young Marine. D'ja do it wid dat machine gon of yourn?'

Nathaniel nodded.

'Good work, my son. For did not our Lord say; "March against Babylon. Pursue, kill, and completely destroy dem, as I have commanded yez. Let da battle cry be heard in da land, a shout of great destruction". Jeremiah 50:21-22.'

Nathaniel smiled.

'So what next, good peoples?' Asked the priest.

'I've promised to take Tom and Louise to find their parents. Not far, few miles away. Then I'd like to get this booty in the house to the abbey where we're all staying.'

'Easily done,' said the priest. 'First den, we gets a good night sleep. Den tomorrow we saddle up some horses for you three peoples. I'll stay here and guard de place from vagabonds and suchlike. When yez come back we'll load da goodies on da wagon and be off.'

'So they have horses and wagons?' Asked Nathaniel.

'Oh yes dey does,' confirmed O'Hara. 'Lots of da beasties.'

'Sounds good,' agreed the Marine. 'I'll take first watch. You two get some sleep. Father, your time is your own.'

'Tanks be ta you, young soldier. I tink dat I'll sit up for a while. Dey has got a lovely lot of wines and whiskeys in da cellar dat I was incarcerated and I shall partake and sit wid youse.'

Father O'Hara picked up one of the church candles, lit it with his lighter and wandered back down the stairs into the cellar. The two teenagers grabbed some blankets and went through to the sitting room and lay down on two of the sofas. Not wanting to stray too far from the Marine and his comforting presence. Within moments they had both fallen into an exhausted slumber.

O'Hara came up from the cellar carrying four wine bottles in his ham-sized mitts. He put them down on the dining room table, went through to the kitchen and returned with two glasses and a corkscrew. He opened two of the bottles and poured Nathaniel a glass without asking. He slid it across and then fished a pack of cigarettes from his breast pocket. Again, without offering, he lit two and handed one to the Marine.

Nathaniel inhaled with great pleasure and nodded his thanks.

'Dere be a huge number of dees in da cellar,' said the priest. 'Most be fifty cartons at least. Now, boyo, what brings you here? Tell da father yourn story and den, if dere be time, I shall regale you wid mine.'

So Nathaniel told his story. He didn't mean to go into the details that he did, but the father was a professional listener and knew exactly when and how to keep the Marine talking. Within a few hours he had extracted Nathaniel's entire life story up until the killing in the church and the second bottle of wine was almost empty and the priest had collected a carton of cigarettes. The room was blue with smoke and the two candles flickered their orange light across the walls and chased shadows across the wood beamed ceiling.

'So, Father,' said the Marine. 'Do you think that God is punishing us?'

'No, Nathaniel. He'll not be punishing us, He is testing us. Oh, to be sure, ours is a vengeful God and humanity is, when it comes down to it, a fairly useless fecking bunch. But our Lord he does love us, worthless sinners dat we be. Now you get yourself some shuteye, Marine. The good father will keep a lookout for yez.'

Nathaniel pulled a blanket from the pile, lay on the carpet and went to sleep.

***

The next morning Nathaniel rose before the sun. Father O'Hara hadn't slept and sat where he had been the night before. Two empty packs of cigarettes and three empty wine bottles bore testament to his cast iron constitution.

'Top of the morning to yez, Marine,' he greeted. Nathaniel nodded a greeting, scrabbled for a cigarette and lit up. Then he went through to the sitting room and woke the teenagers up.

They awoke bright eyed and bushy tailed as only the young can.

They breakfasted on tinned beans heated up in the fireplace, washed down with mineral water and strong black coffee.

Afterwards Father O'Hara took them to the stables. All in all there were six horses. The feed bins were full of oats and there was plenty of hay. The tack room had sufficient saddlery for all of the mounts. Around the back of the stables were two old, reconditioned Dray wagons. Open tops with four tyres and leaf suspension. Probably ten foot by five foot, each with a set of harnesses for two horses.

Tom and Louise saddled five of the horses, one for each of them, excluding O'Hara who was staying to guard the stash, and two extra for their parents.

They mounted up and set off at a fast walk. After half an hour or so Nathaniel spoke.

'Listen up, guys,' he said. 'I want you both to be prepared for the worst. I don't want to be the kiss of death or anything, I hope and pray that all will be fine. But just in case, anything could have happened. Your folks may not be there, they could have moved on, gotten ill, hurt themselves. Just prepare and be strong.'

They both nodded solemnly at him and he could see that they held no false hopes.

It took them a little under four hours to travel the twenty miles to the teenager's parent's house. It was a massive Georgian pile set well back on a country road. Steel gates that looked as if they had never been shut, a marble chip driveway and no perceivable neighbours.

The house itself was white, covered in ivy and in need of some repair. Old money on a slow genteel slide to ruin.

They dismounted and tied the horses to the stone balustrade that ran along the front of the house. Nathaniel waved the two teenagers behind him as they mounted the steps. The front door was closed but unlocked and they walked in, pausing for a second or so in order to let their eyes adjust to the dim interior.

The two teenagers pushed past Nathaniel, calling out for their parents. The Marine followed them as they went from room to room, a sitting room, drawing room, dining room. They found the mother in the library. She was lying on the floor, on her side.

She was alive. Nathaniel knelt down next to her, lifted her head and put his water bottle to her lips. She sipped, swallowed, gagged and then drank fervently. Her eyes flickered open and a smile spread across her face.

'My darlings,' she whispered. 'Is this real?'

Tom grabbed her hand and Louise started weeping.

'Mummy,' said Tom. 'We're here. You'll be safe now.'

'Where's daddy?' Asked Louise.

'I'm so sorry, my darlings,' she said. 'So sorry.'

'What, mummy?' Demanded Louise. 'What's wrong?'

'Daddy died last week,' she said. 'His asthma. I'm so sorry.'

'But what's wrong with you, mummy?' Asked Tom.

'Silly me. All my fault. Daddy had an attack and his pump had run out. So I ran upstairs to look for another. But I slipped. Fell. I think that I've broken my hips. It's taken me two days to crawl here from the bottom of the steps and now that I'm here I do wonder why I bothered. No water here. No water there.'

Nathaniel held the bottle to her lips again and she drank greedily. Then she held out her hand to the Marine. 'Marjorie Stepford,' she said.

Nathaniel took her hand and squeezed it slightly. 'Pleased to meet you, ma'am,' he said. 'Master gunnery sergeant Nathaniel Hogan, United States Marine Corp, at your service.'

She smiled through her pain and Nathaniel felt his heart go out to her. To her bravery, her composure. Her essential Britishness.

'Well, master sergeant, I've always said, if you want something done then call on a non-commissioned officer, preferably a sergeant. So, taking care of my children are you?'

The Marine nodded. 'I am, ma'am.'

'Good,' she nodded. 'Well done.'

Tom started to weep, silently.

'No, no,' Marjorie admonished him. 'That simply won't do, Thomas. Can't go around weeping at everything, goodness me, what would people think?'

Tom held his chin up. 'Sorry, mummy.'

'Now, give mummy a hug, both of you, and then I want you to leave me alone with the master sergeant for a while. Okay?'

The two teenagers hugged their mother and kissed her and then left the room, obeying her wishes.

Nathaniel knelt down next to her again.

'Sergeant Hogan,' she said. 'I have broken both of my hips. I cannot move my legs and I can feel that some sort of infection has set in. Now, I'm not sure what has happened to the civilized world but I do know that it seems to no longer exist. Am I correct in that assumption?'

Nathaniel nodded. 'There has been some sort of solar flare. The electromagnetic waves caused by it have destroyed the world's electrical and electronic goods. Essentially, ma'am, we are back in the dark ages.'

Marjorie nodded. 'Thought as much. So, the only thing left for me would be a long, slow, agonising death.'

Nathaniel showed her the respect of not lying. 'Yes, ma'am. At best case scenario. Might not be so long. We cannot operate, cannot replace the hips, don't even have a decent supply of painkillers.'

'Fine. Now, sergeant, be an absolute sweetheart. Go upstairs, third door on the left you will find a bedroom. Go inside, the next door is a bathroom en suite. Medicine cabinet inside. Take a look and you will find a bottle of Xanax. After that, go to the drawing room, in the corner you will see a liquor cabinet. Bring a bottle of Cognac.' She patted Nathaniel on the hand. 'Hurry now, sergeant. No time for dilly-dallying.'

The Marine did as he was asked, opening the bottle of cognac as he walked back into the room. He handed both the pills and the alcohol over to Marjorie. She prized the cap off the unopened bottle of Xanax and proceeded to swallow them with the cognac, taking five or so at a time until the bottle was finished, breathing deeply as she did so in order to not cough from the spirit intake.

When the pills were finished she struggled her way through half of the bottle of cognac and then beckoned Nathaniel to her.

'My husband died in the kitchen a few days back. Don't let the children see the body, I'm sure that he looks well past his best by now.' Nathaniel nodded. 'I'm not sure how quickly this cocktail works so, please send the children in. It's time for me to say goodbye.'

Nathaniel stood up, faced the lady of the house and saluted. 'I wish that we could have met under better circumstances, ma'am,' he said.

'As do I, master sergeant,' she replied. 'As do I.'

Nathaniel went through to the entrance hall and told the two teenagers that their mother wanted to see them. Then he went outside, sat on the balustrade, lit a cigarette and waited.

After half an hour the two siblings walked out of the front door.

Louise strode up to the Marine and slapped him, hard, across the face. Nathaniel saw it coming but didn't move.

'She's dead,' said Louise. 'She's dead and you could have prevented it. You gave her the pills, you killed her.' She slapped the Marine again.

Nathaniel shook his head. 'She was a very brave lady, Louise. She knew that she was beyond cure and she did the right thing. Seeing you and Tom before she went was a gift beyond all that she could have hoped for. I am really, really sorry for your loss, but I did not kill your mother and I would never do anything to hurt either of you.' He stepped forward and put his arms around Louise and hugged her. She burst into tears and clung to him, her breath coming in short ragged bursts.

Tom stood to the side, his eyes red rimmed but tearless, obeying his mother's last wishes. No tears, no crying, after all, what would people think.

Nathaniel reached out and pulled Tom into an embrace with his sister.

'It's alright, my boy,' he said. 'You can cry. There's no shame in tears. None at all.'

So the two teenagers cried for the loss of their family. And their world and all that they had ever known.

And the big Marine held them tight and kept them safe.

Chapter 29

Janice had been sleeping rough for five days now and then, last night, she had lost her blanket. She had been sleeping next to a thin hedge alongside the road when two men had grabbed her, waking her as they pulled her from the blanket and started to tear her shirt off. She had kicked out, twisting and screaming and then she had run, pausing only briefly to snatch up her doctors bag.

Now she had no idea where she was as the map book had been lying next to her when she slept. During the day she had come across a village that had been burned to the ground. She had thought to search it for food but as she got closer she could see that the ground was covered in bodies and she couldn't force herself to go any closer. She searched every car that she came across and, in the late afternoon, she found a tin of sweetcorn and a box of Tampons under the passenger seat of an old Rover. She put the Tampons into her bag and opened the tin using one of her scalpels. It was one of the finest meals that she could ever remember eating.

She was constantly thirsty, although she filled her water bottle whenever she could, water butts, streams and even puddles, but she knew that she was slowly dehydrating, her heartbeat was up, she hadn't urinated for over six hours and her mouth and lips were constantly dry.

The sun was going down and she had to find shelter for the night. Preferably some sort of natural protection, as a barn or house would attract people. And Janice no longer trusted people. After walking for a while she saw what looked like a good spot. A clump of thick bushes in amongst a copse of trees, the vegetation thick enough to dull the cutting wind and to conceal from prying eyes.

She only noticed the gray sheet of plastic once she had worked her way into the middle of the thick patch of greenery. It had been artfully concealed with mud and leaves, low to the ground but skillfully erected so as to provide maximum shelter.

She froze, unsure as whether to turn and run or to investigate further. She squatted down and waited for a while. The minutes ticked by and she heard nothing so she edged forward, slowly, and peeked inside the bivouac.

Lying on his back was a young man dressed in a dirty army uniform. Next to him was a plastic shopping bag containing a couple of full water bottles and three cans of food. She couldn't see exactly what the cans contained because their labels were burned off. The right side of the soldier's face was covered with a blood soaked bandage that had been roughly applied. Janice couldn't tell if he was alive or dead.

She crawled over to him and took his pulse, feeling for it in the side of his neck. He was alive but the pulse was weak and ragged. His breathing so shallow as to be almost impossible to detect.

Janice opened one of the water bottles and drank deeply from it. Her eyes started to water and the sheer pleasure of imbibing the pure liquid made her feel giddy. She drank almost half of the bottle before her thirst was slaked.

Then she opened her doctor's bag and started to lay out her instruments. First, she removed the bloodied bandage from the soldier's head, shuddering as it revealed his wound.

He had obviously taken a shotgun round from close range. The pellets had torn out his eye and lacerated the flesh on the right side of his face. She could see four or five of the pellets were still embedded in him, and bits of skin and flesh hung in ragged strips from his cheek, like pieces of red ribbon. The fact that he was still alive was proof of an almost inhuman fortitude.

So Janice set to work, knowing that she had to do what she could, but also knowing that there was less than little chance that this brave young man would last the night.

She worked as fast as she could and by the time the light had failed she had removed the pellets, stitched and glued the tattered flesh, given him a shot of broad-spectrum antibiotics and bandaged the wound. Then she tilted his head forward and spent a while dribbling water into his mouth and ensuring that he swallowed it.

Finally, she lay down next to him, spread her jacket over the both of them and moved as close as she could to keep him warm. She was asleep within minutes secure that she was well hidden from passers by.

When she awoke the next morning the young man was sitting up next to her, sipping water from one of the bottles.

'Good morning,' he said. 'So, I'm not dead.'

Janice smiled. 'It would appear so,' she replied.

'I can feel that you've done some work on my face. Are you a nurse?'

'Doctor,' said Janice. 'I cleaned your wound, took the shot out, stitched and made good. But I'm afraid that your eye is gone. And I'm no plastic surgeon, you aren't going to be entering any more beauty pageants.'

The soldier grinned. 'Damn, there goes my dream of becoming miss universe.' He held out his hand. 'Thank you. My name is Axel.'

She took it. 'Janice. Pleased to meet you.'

'I wonder if I could bother you for some pain killers, doc?' Asked Axel. 'I must say, the old face hurts like buggery.'

Janice scrambled through her bag, pulled out a bottle and offered Axel some codeine capsules.

'Right,' he said after swallowing them. 'Not sure what your plan is but we need to keep moving. First we breakfast on a tin of beans then keep searching, foraging. To stay is to die.'

'I'm looking for my parents,' said Janice. 'They live in Tempsford.'

'Where's that?'

Janice waved her hand in a vague Northerly direction. 'Lost my map. Not that sure. Whenever I drove to see them I had a satnav. So I simply followed instructions, never really took in the actual directions themselves.'

'Okay,' said Axel. 'We head that way,' he also waved towards the North.

They both laughed. Then he opened the can of beans using the ring-pull on the top. He fished a spoon out of his pocket and offered Janice, who ate first. She allowed herself a third of the can. The soldier finished off the rest. Then he packed his plastic sheet, water bottles and empty tin into his rucksack and they set off across the fields. At times they saw individuals or couples roaming the countryside and they simply ignored them and kept walking.

However, the one time they saw a large group in the distance and Axel made them hide in a depression in the landscape, gray plastic covering them. Invisible. Discretion was the better part of valor, he told her. And bands of any size were best avoided.

Late afternoon they found a tiny trickle of a steam, filled their water bottles up and drank until their stomachs felt distended. Axel also spent some time pulling tender leaves off a Hawthorn tree. Next he attacked a patch of pretty white flowers, pulling them up by the roots and washing them off in the stream. When Janice got closer he showed her what looked like a handful of anemic carrots.

'Queen Anne's lace,' he said. 'Wild carrots. Also, Hawthorn leaves instead of bread. Now there's two of us, we need to substantially increase our supply of food.' He pushed the forage into his rucksack. 'Come on. Let's keep moving.'

They continued north until the sky began to darken. Janice noticed that Axel was starting to stumble a little as he walked, grimacing at the pain. Once again, with a soldier's feel, he found a spot that they could conceal themselves for the night.

He built his small bivouac and opened a tin of beans. He used the other empty tin to halve the supply and then he chopped the wild carrot up small and mixed it in. Then, using his spoon, he showed Janice to put a spoonful of the bean and carrot onto a Hawthorn leaf, roll it like a mini fajita and eat. Janice was impressed, the leaves were slightly peppery and the carrots imparted a fresh crunch.

Before the light faded she changed his bandage and injected him with the last of her antibiotics. She didn't say anything to him but the wound wasn't looking good. Despite her best efforts an infection had started to set in and, already, the stitches were pulled tight, the ruined flesh red and puffy. She needed more antibiotics, much more. Also antibiotic powder and fresh sterile bandages.

The next morning when they awoke, Axel was shivering with the onset of fever. She gave him water and paracetemol and they started to walk, but Janice could see that the young soldier was taking immense strain. Every couple of steps he would stop and shiver uncontrollably and the side of his face had swollen alarmingly.

However, there was little she could do and rest would not slow the infection. Their only choice was to continue and hope for a miracle of some sort.

Late that afternoon the two of them walked around a copse of trees to come face-to-face with five men. Two of the men were carrying shotguns. The others carried baseball bats.

And Janice knew that her prayers for a miracle had gone the other way as the one man ran forward and hammered Axel across the head, knocking him to the ground.

Chapter 30

The first thing that they had done when they arrived back at the hamlet and greeted father O'Hara was to tell him what had transpired. Then the priest had taken them all outside and made them stand together under a vast old Oak tree. He told them to bow their heads and spend a moment in silence thinking about the departed mother and father. Then he said a simple prayer.

'O God, who hast commanded us to honor our father and our mother;

in Thy mercy have pity on the souls of my father and mother,

and forgive them their trespasses;

and make me to see them again in the joy of everlasting brightness.

Through Christ our Lord. Amen.'

They loaded everything that they could onto the two flat back wagons. Nathaniel had started with the medicines, then weapons and ammunitions, then the food, candles, blankets, clothes. Finally the cigarettes and then whatever space was left, he had assured father O'Hara that he could fill it with alcohol. They weren't much bothered with the bottled water as it was heavy and the abbey had a well.

The priest had loaded the hard tack first. Whisky and brandy. Then port and finally wine. But there were still hundreds and hundreds of bottles of wine left in the cellar, a fact that thoroughly upset the holy man.

He kept shaking his head and muttering. 'Tis a terrible ting ta leave da alcohol here for bandits. What wid me being a man of God, married to the holy ghost an all dat, de only pleasures dat I can partake in is da smoking and da drinkin.' Then he crossed himself. 'An da prayin of course. Great pleasure I gets in da praying to our Lord.'

He took his lit candle down into the cellar for one last look. 'Come on,' he beckoned to Nathaniel. 'A final look-see in case we missed sumat special. Give us a hand wid dose young eyes of yourn.'

Hogan smiled and followed the priest, lighting another candle as he descended the steps. The cellar ran under the entire length of the huge house and there seemed to be no system behind its layout. It was simply scores of shelves with hundreds of bottles on them.

Hogan heard the father exclaim joyously.

'Rehoboam. Ardeg.'

'Sorry, father. Is that Latin?'

'Hebrew and Gaelic, my son. A rehoboam is a large bottle dat contains six normal size bottles in it. Ardeg is a single malt whisky from Islay. An dats what I's found. A great big bottle of Ardeg. Found it in da corner covered in dust. Does a favor an check da corners for more, would yez?'

'Okay, father,' replied Nathaniel. 'But let's make it quick. I want to be back well before nightfall.'

'Less talky more looky,' responded father O'Hara.

Nathaniel held the candle up and checked in the corner closest to him. Empty. He strode quickly across to the opposite corner and checked there to find the same. But, as he turned away, he fancied that he had seen something. Something tall and hidden in so much dust as to be more a hint of an object than the actual object itself. He took his candle closer.

It was propped up in the corner. Dust lay thick upon it like a protective blanket. But there was no hiding the shape. It stood around four foot high, the butterfly shaped double blades at least eighteen inches wide. The oak shaft two inches across and covered in brass studs. The handle covered in strips of wound leather.

He reached out and freed it from its prison of dust and dereliction. His hands were shaking and, as he touched it, it was as if a song of joy had started in his head. It was the self-same axe that he had seen in his dream about the druids. The dream that had left him with his scar. The Marine tapped the weapon against the wall and the dust fell off to reveal the blades in their full glory. Simple and unadorned, the edges still glowed sharp as newly forged steel and, as he swung it back and forth a few times, the haft was as flexible as newly bound.

'No whisky here, father,' he called out, his voice hoarse with emotion. 'Let's go.' He headed up the stairs, carrying the battle-axe with him.

Louise was in charge of the one wagon with its two horses and father O'Hara the other. Nathaniel and Tom had a horse each. The Marine swung into the saddle and slotted the axe into one of the saddle straps, the head nestled alongside the saddle.

'Wow,' said Tom. 'Cool axe.'

Nathaniel grinned. 'I thought so.'

They set off back to the abbey, the Marine riding next to father O'Hara's wagon and Tom next to his sister's.

'So tell me, father,' said Nathaniel. 'Was this your parish?'

'Nay. Dis has nay bin a church for many a year now. We sold it to de people of dis heathen hamlet some two-year back. Actually, my poor church has been selling a lot of property of late. The Holy Father sent me on a tour to unconsecrate all of de churches in this area and surrounds. Some seven in all. Well, I's been on da road for but one day when da Lord decided, in his wisdom, to return us all to da dark ages. For some few days, or maybe more, I wus totally lost, my son. Not biblically, yez see, only physically. Den I did find my way here, guided by prayer and da odd direction from strangers. I figured, just because all had gone to pot, twas no reason why I shouldn't still be doing my job. So here I wuz, sent to unconsectrate de building. I arrived and dey was all nice as pie. Oh, father have some tea and a drap of the good stuff. Oh, an here be a cigar for you as well. Den da moment I finish de rite of deconsecration da feckin bastards smack me onna head wid a hunk oh wood and bundle me in da cellar wid only de booze and de cigarettes as my company. Dat was some tree day ago or so.'

O'Hara lit himself a cigarette and then glanced back at the two teenagers. They had fallen behind a little and were out of earshot.

'Now be telling me, Marine. Da chillun's mamy. From what you say she be killin herself den. Takin her own life?'

Nathaniel thought a while before he answered. 'Why?'

'Well,' continued father O'Hara. 'It be a mortal sin and all. And assisting be a mortal sin as well. Our Lord gets extra riled at dose two tings, yez see. Awful hard to get into da kingdom of eternal light if yez committed a mortal sin.'

'What are the mortal sins?'

O'Hara shook his head. 'Oh, even on dis long trip dere be top many to list. It's hard work being a catholic, my son.'

'What about murder?'

'Oh yes, dat one is plain.'

'So by killing those Satanists at the church I committed a mortal sin?'

'No. Yez committed a righteous act, my son. A soldier of de Lord.'

'What about booze and cigarettes. You know that cigs give you cancer and booze messes up your liver. So aren't you slowly killing yourself? Isn't that a mortal sin?'

O'Hara laughed. 'Don't bandy words wid da Lord, soldier. But to answer, no, dat is mere stupidity. And da Lord knows dat is no sin.'

'Well then,' said Nathaniel. 'When Marjorie asked for the pills and the brandy she had no idea that the mix would kill her. She was merely looking for a way to ease her pain.'

'I see. And youze? Did youze know?'

Nathaniel shook his head.

'Ah, and, as I already said,' continued the priest. 'Bieng stupid tis no sin. Good den. In da name of de Lord I exonerate youze boat.' O'Hara breathed a sigh of relief. 'Dat feels good. Much happier now dat de whole mortal sin thing is put to rest.'

He lit two cigarettes, leaned over and handed one to the Marine.

Nathaniel saluted him with it and they continued on their way.

They arrived at the gates of the abbey like conquering heroes. They brought the wagons in and literally everyone came to the quadrangle to see them. The Prof was introduced to father O'Hara and then he organized the scholars to take all of the food to the kitchens, the weapons to the armory and the blankets and candles to the storerooms. The nurse took care of the medicines herself.

That night, before they ate, father O'Hara stood up and said grace.

Nathaniel smiled. Their little enclave of survivors had just got bigger by one.

Chapter 31

Axel lay groaning on the ground so the man hit him again. A solid blow that sounded like wood being chopped.

Janice screamed and one of the other men slapped her so hard that she too fell over. The man who had slapped her put his shotgun on the ground and started to unbuckle his belt and take down his trousers.

'Hey, Conrad,' said one of the other men. 'Why are you going first? You went first yesterday.'

Conrad tuned to face the complainer. 'Stuff you, Jervis. I always go first. That's because I'm the oldest brother. I go first, Jackson goes second, you go third and the twins draw straws. I told you already. That's the way it happens.'

'But you and Jackson get the shotguns as well. It's not fair.'

Conrad pulled his trousers up, stepped over to Jervis and slapped him. 'Not fair? You little wanker. It's not about fair. You do as you're told or you don't get any more pussy. Do you want that? Have to jerk off while we all get the good stuff?'

Jervis shook his head. 'Sorry, Conrad.'

'Yeah well now you go after the twins. You go last as punishment. Okay?'

Jervis sniveled. 'Okay, Conrad. Sorry.'

Conrad turned back to Janice, dropping his trousers once again. 'Oh yes,' he said. 'This is going to be sweet.'

There was a crack of an assault rifle and the front of Conrad's chest exploded in a red mist. He didn't even have time to register surprise before his brain shut down and he fell to the floor, dead.

There was another flurry of shots and Janice could see the bullets striking the other men. Jervis sprang up and started to run but was cut down by a volley of fire before he had taken three steps.

A large man with a long black beard and carrying a rifle ran up and knelt beside Janice. 'Are you all right?' He asked.

Janice stared at him and then started to weep.

He put his one arm around her. 'Don't cry, little one,' he said. 'You are safe now. Papa Dante and his boys will take care of you.'

There were six men including Papa Dante and four of them carried Axel gently back to a ring of caravans.

Papa led Janice, holding her by the elbow. When they got to the caravans an old woman approached them. She pulled the dressings from Axel's face and ran her fingers tenderly across his features, stopping every now and then to concentrate. Then told the men to carry him to her vardo.

'He's suffering from pyrexia brought on by pyogenic infection. Possibly staph or strep,' said Janice.

The old lady looked at Janice and smiled and Janice noticed, for the first time, that the old woman was blind. 'Go have tea,' she said. 'I will fix your boyfriend.'

'He's not my boyfriend,' said Janice.

The old woman raised an eyebrow. 'Not yet. Now go, I am busy.'

'But, with all due respect. How can you? You're blind. I have to stay with him.'

Papa took Janice by the arm. 'Come, my pretty. Leave Gogo to do what Gogo does.'

Papa Dante led the doctor to his vardo. He helped Janice up the steps, then he introduced her to his wife. But first he asked her name.

'Janice,' she answered and, for the first time since she could remember she didn't add the ubiquitous 'Doctor' on the end.

'Well, Janice, this is Mama, my wife and my love and the second most beautiful person in the world.'

'Only the second?' Asked Mama. 'Who is

the first then, you old philanderer?'

Papa Dante shrugged. 'Who knows, Mama. I for one have never met them but are you so arrogant as to assume that there is no one in the entire universe that might be just a little more beautiful than you?'

Mama punched the big man in the arm. 'You are a pedant, sir. A pedagogue and a dogmatist.'

'Aye,' agreed Papa. 'And also a liar. You are the most beautiful women in the world.'

Janice laughed and the husband and wife laughed with her.

Mama went outside and came back with a kettle that she rested on a counter top. Then she busied herself with mugs and tea and sugar. She didn't ask how Janice took her tea she simply made it strong and sweet and then chucked a decent dram of rum into it.

Janice held the mug with both hands and breathed in the fragrant steam. Eventually she took a sip. It was beyond delicious and the sugar and alcohol stopped her shaking and calmed her nerves.

Then Mama handed her a sandwich. It was made from rough baked bread and on it were wedges of smoky ham and ripe cheddar cheese. Janice ate like she was starving, which she was and as she finished Mama pushed another one into her hand. The doctor felt like crying with appreciation and her eyes welled up with emotion. But Mama simply patted her on the back and gestured for her to keep eating.

After she had consumed the food Janice felt an enormous lethargy envelop her. The savagery of the last few days caught up with her and the feeling of real safety and warmth and welcome washed over her and she fell into a deep sleep.

Papa Dante waited until her breathing was deep and regular and then he laid her out on the sofa, covered her with a feather eiderdown, closed the shutters and left her to rest.

Papa walked into Gogo's vardo and flinched. The stench was awful. The old lady was mashing up a poultice in a marble pestle and Papa could identify some of the ingredients. Garlic, ginger, honey…and then the rest was too strange to contemplate. It looked like some sort of crushed dried insect or bug. But whatever it was, the smell was eye-watering.

The soldier was still unconscious, lying on his back on Gogo's table that she used to treat everyone. Papa noticed that she had removed the lad's stitches and his wounds were open and suppurating lymph and pus.

Then Gogo took a shoebox out of her

chest of drawers, opened it and grabbed a handful of what looked like cotton candy. Papa knew, from experience, that it was actually spider webs, collected just after the morning dew had dried up and the webs were at their cleanest and newest. She then rolled the web into various lengths and began to pack Axel's wounds. When she was satisfied that a wound was sufficiently packed she would squeeze it closed and the natural adhesive qualities of the web would keep it perfectly sealed.

After that she covered the side of his face in the evil-smelling warm poultice, tucked a blanket around him for warmth and then left the vardo, gesturing for Papa to follow.

'So, Gogo,' said Papa. 'Will he live?'

The old lady nodded. 'If he is lucky. Even a few more hours and he would have been beyond repair. But I have extended his life, for now. But he needs real medicine, antibiotics. Huge amounts or he will relapse and succumb.'

Gogo spoke with no false modesty, nor was she boasting of her prowess. She merely stated the facts. She was confident that, using ingredients found in fields and surrounds, she had pushed back the inevitable, but she was just as sure that the relief was not permanent. Axel has been given time, just not much of it.

Janice woke in the early evening and Mama

gave her a large mug of soup that was so thick as to almost be a stew.

'I cannot thank you enough,' said the doctor. 'Your kindness and generosity in a world of madness is almost incomprehensible.'

Mama shrugged. 'You were lucky. The boys were looking for one of the horses that had bolted and they heard your scream.'

'Yes,' agreed Janice. 'I was lucky. But, over the last few days I have seen people attack each other over a can of soda. People who wouldn't let me shelter in their house through fear. I have been attacked twice and I came across a village that had been burned to the ground and was full of dead people. Yet, without thought, you have taken me in.'

'Aye,' said Papa Dante. Janice hadn't heard the big man enter and she flinched in surprise. 'Sorry, little one,' he continued. 'I didn't mean to shock you. I just wanted to say that your boyfriend is resting easy. I am sure that we shall see vast improvement by tomorrow.'

'Thank you,' said Janice, not bothering to deny her alleged relationship with Axel.

'Do you see that?' Papa Dante pointed at a small ceramic plaque on the wall of the vardo, next to the window. Janice lent forward and read it aloud to herself.

"The mental age of the average adult Gypsy is thought to be about that of a child of ten. Gypsies have never accomplished anything of great significance in writing, painting, musical composition, science or social organization. Quarrelsome, quick to anger or laughter, they are unthinkingly but not deliberately cruel. Loving bright colors, they are ostentatious and boastful, but lack bravery." Encyclopedia Britannica in 1954.

'That was society's official viewpoint on our people. And that was less than eighty years ago. Still today many people think of us the same way. But what many do not know is that we are a very religious people and has not the Lord told us to care for our fellow man?'

Janice nodded. 'But I have recently learned that our fellow man is a stupid dickhead,' she said.

Both Papa Dante and Mama laughed. 'Truly said, little one, truly said,' agreed Papa. 'I often wonder why God saw fit to limit man's intelligence but to still allow him limitless stupidity. Now, I know that you have been a bed all day, but I want you to drink this,' Papa poured a shot of rum into a mug. 'And then snuggle back into that there eiderdown and get some more sleep. Sleep heals much and you shall find that, by tomorrow, life will contain more joy and less…stupid dickheads.'

Janice downed the rum, lay back and, within minutes was asleep again.

Chapter 32

Commander Ammon had left the thinnest line of defense that he dared. A mere seven hundred battle Orcs, fifty trolls, five hundred goblin archers and around five hundred constructs to supply arrows, water and replace broken weapons. He had also placed four much smaller groups of warriors on the passes through the mountains that the Elven tribes had used to get through into the realm.

There was little, if no chance at all, that any of these defenders would make it through the gateway to the new world. But they all knew that. He had not asked for volunteers. He had simply instructed and they had obeyed. This was not bravery nor was it patriotism, it was merely inbred discipline. The Orcs, trolls, goblins and constructs had been selectively bred for many, many generations so as to be refined into the perfect tools for their particular job.

Orcs stood around five feet ten inches high, weighed three hundred plus pounds. Massively thick bones and two-inch thick gray hide. Eyes deep set to avoid injury, no discernable ears to get ripped off, no hair to hold on to and their noses little more than two holes in their face covered by skin flaps. Their large jaws were lined with rows of sharp canines and their three fingered hands sported long black talons, razor sharp talons. In short, they were perfect killing machines.

Goblins, however, were much sorter. Five feet tall, short bowlegs that caused them to waddle when they walked. Large eyes capable of seeing almost as well in the dark as in daylight. Long arms that reached almost to the floor and hugely overdeveloped chest and back muscles. Thus a five foot tall Goblin was capable of firing a six foot long recurved bow.

The trolls were little more than massive, twelve-foot tall, mountains of muscle. Slow witted and just capable of following commands, they were an unstoppable force when used correctly. Their ten-foot shields and twenty-foot pikes capable not only of forming a defensive wall but also of delivering a crushing advance.

Seth and the rest of the twelve mages that formed the magik-high-commission had formed a magik circle on a huge plain behind the city. There they had fasted for three days and they traveled collectively to the planet Earth and the destination, the stone circle in

Cornwall. And now they were creating the gateway to their new world.

The physical size of the gateway would be in the region of six yards across by two yards high. Thus the population would have to file through the opening, marching five abreast. The column of refugees together with the orc-drawn wagons and the piles of supplies would be over twenty leagues long and would take around five days and nights to get through completely.

This meant that Ammon and his troops had to keep the Elven hordes off their backs for another few days.

Ammon heard Seth's voice in his head as the mage far-spoke him.

'Not long, commander. I think that you should begin to ready the populace. In a couple more hours we will have coalesced enough energy to open the portal.'

Ammon pulsed a thought of thanks back and strode off to ready the first wave of Orcs and goblins that would go through the gateway in force, in order to secure the area for the rest.

Chapter 33

Basel Ratford, the old commander in chief of the Belmarsh boys, was dead. Patrick's rifle shot had blown off the back part of the chief's foot, septicemia had set in within hours and by the end of the next day he was too weak to move.

So, in a show of human kindness and compassion, the Belmarsh boys had decided that anyone who was too pathetic to even feed themselves was far too feeble to be their leader and they decided to vote for a new one, leaving Basel to die slowly from dehydration.

The voting had turned into a full scale brawl and eventually, after three deaths, a monster of a man know to all as Ratfink, real name Jonathan Naybor, mass murderer and habitual steroid taker, became the next commander in chief. Unlike the former chief however, Naybor was an educated man. He had gained a history degree from Essex University before his lifetime incarceration and, in the last twelve years of his imprisonment, he had, through the Open University, garnered honors and a master's degree in history and then a doctorate in Philosophy.

Officially he was J. Naybor MA (Hist) Ph.D AKA Ratfink AKA Commander in Chief the Belmarsh Boys.

He was a staunch follower of the Giovanni Gentile School of fascist philosophy. And saw himself as a cross between Mussolini, Hitler and Julius Caesar. Like many habitual murderers, he suffered from massive delusions of grandeur combined with clinical paranoia and megalomania. Up until the pulse, these delusions were being controlled by the ingestion of industrial quantities of Respiridone antipsychotic medication. Now, however, his psychosis was allowed full rein.

Already he had reorganized the structure of the Belmarsh boys. Under him he had nominated three Vice Presidents. All of them had master degrees. One he put in charge of enforcement or private body guarding and internal discipline. The second in charge of the army, or external discipline and the third in charge of what he called civics. Food, clothing shelter and organizational structures.

Naybor was not content to simply roam the countryside raping and looting. Not for him the nomadic life of the Mongolian horseman. No, he had decided that he was going to start a true kingdom. And to do that he needed a castle. Some form of physical defense with living quarters for his army and entourage.

That morning the boys had taken over the small village of Twyfram where they had decided to settle in for a few days. A church, a shop, a pub and a few houses. Naybor had stopped the men rampaging through the village, pillaging and destroying. Burned houses and dead citizens didn't help anything. For a king needs subjects and land and water. So what was the point of murdering all of your subjects and burning all of your property to the ground?

So he had appropriated the largest house in the village and now he and his three VPs were poring over a large ordnance survey map that had been unrolled and placed on the dining room table.

The chief was looking for a castle. He pointed at a circle on the map.

'Here,' he said. 'The fortified Abbey of Lilysworth.' He turned to one of his VPs. 'Cody, go and get some locals. I want to know what the hell this abbey place is.'

Cody saluted and headed for the door.

'No, wait,' called Naybor. 'The girls. Kill two birds with one stone. Bring, oh say, five or six of the best looking girls. Young, late teens early twenties.'

The chief walked over to the window and looked out at the view. Rolling downs, hedges, apple trees. All in vivid shades of green. Truly God's own country, he thought. He took a cigarette from a pack, placed it between his lips and waited. A VP leaned over and flicked a flame. The chief inhaled and carried on contemplating the view. His view.

The door opened and Cody led a gaggle of six girls into the room. They huddled into the corner. Afraid.

Naybor gestured to the one closest to him. Short, brunette, shoulder length hair. Blue eyes, large breasts. She shuffled towards him, her feet dragging in trepidation.

'Come on, girl,' he said. 'No need to worry. I mean you no harm. Now, look here,' he pointed at the map. 'This abbey. What do you know about it?'

'It's an old abbey,' she answered, her voice small and tight.

'Obviously,' said Naybor. 'Have you been there?'

She nodded.

'And?' He encouraged her.

'It's big. Got a high wall all round it and a big wooden gate. It's a school as well. Don't know what the school's called.'

'How many students?' Asked the chief. 'Is it a boarding school?'

She nodded. 'About three hundred I

suppose. Maybe more.'

The chief grinned. 'Perfect, absolutely perfect. Accommodation for the boys and more. Fortified, probably got some bloody serious headmaster's house for yours truly. Prefectomundo.'

He swaggered over to the group of girls, his head held high ala Mussolini's el Duce pose.

'Spread out, girls,' he said. 'Your commander in chief wants a gander at you.'

The girls shuffled into a ragged row and the chief walked down it. He paused at the third girl. She was tiny. Little more than a child. Her white t-shirt revealed adolescent breasts and her figure had yet to mature into the curves of womanhood.

'How old are you?' He asked. 'What's your name?'

'Eleven. My name's Tammy.'

'Jesus Christ,' shouted the chief. 'Jesus H Christ. Cody, come here. What the hell is this? Do you think I'm a pedo? A little girl bonker?' He slapped Cody so hard that the VP fell to the floor. The chief kicked him a few times. 'Are you a baby bonker, Cody?' He asked. 'Is that why you chose this child? You know what we do to baby bonkers, don't you?'

'No, chief,' yelled Cody. 'Sorry, chief. My mistake. You said young so I got a spread.

Look,' he pointed at a red haired girl. 'She's maybe thirty-five or so. Young to old. Give you a choice, chief. Sorry.'

'She's eleven, you dick. Eleven.' He kicked Cody again.

Tammy took advantage of the confusion to run for the door. She opened it and disappeared across the fields, running as fast as she could.

'Ah, crap,' growled the chief. 'Now look what you've done. Get up, quickly.' Cody staggered to his feet.

'There,' the chief pointed out of the window at the fleeing girl. 'She's getting away. Shoot her.'

Cody looked puzzled. 'But, chief. If I shoot her then you'll beat me up.'

'No, Cody. If you bonk her I'll kill you. Now shoot the bitch before she gets away. Can't have people flouting the law that way. Just wont do.'

Cody went to the window, drew his nine-millimeter Browning Hi-Power, lined it up and pulled the trigger.

Tammy went down like her legs had been chopped out from under her, disappearing into the long grass.

A couple of the girls screamed.

Naybor held a finger to his lips. 'Shut up.' He cast his gaze along them, taking in the attributes of each one. Finally he spoke.

'Ha, stuff it. I'm the chief, why choose. Cody, get them into the upstairs bedroom, make sure that they're stripped and ready. I'll be up in a few minutes.'

He strode to the window and looked for Tammy's body. But it was hidden in the long grass and was too far away. It had been a good shot. A great shot, actually. He must remember to congratulate Cody. After all, a good leader knew when to be cruel and when to be kind. And he was a good leader, he thought. Perhaps the best ever.

***

Tammy lay in the grass. She hadn't moved since she had tripped while running. The bullet that someone had fired at her had whistled over her head so close that it had actually flicked up a piece of her hair.

Her mother had always laughed at her clumsiness but this time, falling over had saved her life.

With great patience the young girl crawled through the long grass, working her way towards the woods. She had two things in her mind; firstly, get away from the terrible gang of men that had taken over the village. Secondly, warn the abbey that the gang was coming. She had been to the abbey before to listen to a music recital and she had liked both the place and the people. Especially the old professor who was the headmaster of the school.

In the back of her mind she did have a third concern. Tammy did not actually live in the village, she had gone on school holidays with her friend Rebecca and had no idea where her parents or her older brother, Marcus, were. Or even if they were still alive. But she had forced all thoughts of them from her mind in order to concentrate solely on survival.

After forty minutes of careful crawling she got to the edge of the forest and scuttled into the shelter of the trees. It took her a while to orientate herself and, once she had, she jogged off in, what she hoped was, the direction of the abbey.

That night she slept under a bush. Six hours of fits and starts. As the sun rose, so did she. She spent the first ten minutes sucking the dew off leaves to assuage her thirst. It worked better than she had hoped although it did leave a slightly bitter taste in her mouth. Then she continued her slow jog towards the abbey, keeping her eyes skinned for any strangers.

Around mid day she came across a small spring and she lay on her stomach, put her mouth into the water and drank until she felt fit to burst. By now her feet were a mass of blisters and she was exhausted. Although she was a fit young girl and had even been a member of the school track team; she had little body fat and had not eaten for two days now. To keep going, her body was now processing its own muscle fiber. Eating itself in a self-destructive need for energy.

Tammy could no longer jog and decided to walk fast for twenty steps then walk slowly for the next twenty, then rest for ten seconds. She kept this up for two hours before the ten-second rest became twenty seconds. Then a minute and, finally, she simply crawled to a clump of bushes on the side of the road and fell into an exhausted coma-like sleep.

She was awoken just after first light by the sound of people talking. She was too terrified to move lest someone see her so she could not get a look at them. She lay as still as death and waited. If she heard a female voice, she told herself, then she would reveal herself, but she had learned of late that groups of males were not to be trusted.

Twenty minutes later she heard a rattle of gunfire and knew that she had made the correct decision remaining hidden. She stayed curled up under the bushes for another hour, shivering as waves of fear and exhaustion washed over her. When she finally ventured out and started to walk again, every step was agony as the blisters on her feet burst and bled and the lack of liquids ensured that her joints and muscles were stiff and painful due to the surfeit of lactic acid that her dehydrated body could no longer drain away.

By the early evening she was still walking, one ragged step after the other. A simple automotive movement that her exhausted body was carrying out in the same way as she breathed in and out.

She was also starting to hallucinate. Large winged creatures flapped across her vision causing momentary black outs. Tiny undulations in the road became mountains worthy of Lord of the Rings landscapes. Her ears felt as though stuffed with cotton wool.

And then she came to a wall. A wall so tall and so vast as to mean that her journey was at an end. There was no possible way of getting over or around or through such a wall. She stared at the wall for a while. Thinking. And the more that she contemplated it the more she realized that something was wrong. The wall was at a strange angle. Eventually she worked it out and chuckled to herself. She was lying down. She had collapsed at the base of the wall.

It was over. She fluttered in and out of consciousness. Grays and blacks and red spots surged across her vision.

And then a female face. Pale and beautiful and framed with long red hair smiled down at her. And a man lent over her. He was huge and his green eyes sparkled like jewels. He picked her up and cradled her to his chest while the girl stroked her hair. Someone held a water bottle to her lips and she drank, the water coursed through her. The finest champagne, its life giving properties swelling her dehydrated cells, thinning her blood, switching her kidneys back on. Life.

The big man carried her. Walking towards a gate in the huge wall. She felt like she was in a hammock on a ship. Cradled by his arms and safe from the elements.

'They're coming,' she whispered to him. 'They're coming and they're going to kill everyone.'

Nathaniel shook his head and smiled.

'No, my darling,' he said. 'Whoever they are - they're coming and they are going to try to kill everyone. But I won't let that happen.'

And she smiled back at him and fell asleep. Secure in the knowledge that she had done the right thing.

Chapter 34

Papa Dante was impressed. He stood in front of his vardo, unarmed, staring up at the guards on the wall. The large wooden gates in front of him were further protected by rows of wooden stakes that would allow a wagon through but only via a torturous S that meant no one could charge the gates.

Two young men stood on the wall, one armed with a shotgun and the other with what looked like some sort of .22 target rifle. They both had their weapons trained on him. Papa was not offended by this unfriendly gesture. Bad times oft called for bad behavior. And anyway, although neither of the young men on the ramparts knew it, Papa had placed two of his men in the trees and they had their assault rifles trained on the defenders. So, if all went wrong Papa was reasonably confident that his men would fire first. After all, the youngsters on the parapet both looked extremely nervous. And young. Very young. Also Papa had approached in peace looking only for some help with the young injured soldier that they had with them.

Then Papa heard some footsteps behind him. He turned to see a tall man in full combat gear. In his right hand he held an M249M22 machine gun. In his left, clutched together by their barrels, two assault rifles. Two assault rifles that had belonged to his men in the trees. The man dropped the assault rifles and brought the machine gun to bear. Papa noticed that, incongruously, the man also had an old-fashioned battle axe clipped to his belt.

'How ya'll doing?' He asked.

Papa nodded. 'We be doing fine, good sir. We be doing fine.' He pointed at the rifles. 'My men,' he continued. 'Are they?' He drew a finger across his throat.

The soldier shook his head. 'Unconscious. They'll be fine. Wake up with a headache and a bit of embarrassment. Nothing permanent. So how can I help?'

'We have a young man with us,' said Papa Dante. 'Found him and a young lass in less than fortunate circumstances. The young man is a soldier. Looks to be a captain by his uniform. The lady is a doctor. The soldier needs medicine. Antibiotics. We have done what we can but when we saw this place we thought it worth the ask.'

Hogan nodded. 'Show me.'

Papa led him to Gogo's vardo and opened the front door. Hogan peered inside. Axel was lying on the bed. Still unconscious. The poultice had been removed from his wounds and the right side of his face was lightly covered with a silk bandage. But the ravages of his injury were still plain to see.

'Shotgun?' Asked Hogan.

Papa nodded.

'We have antibiotics and everything else that he would need. Wait here, I need to speak to the professor.'

Papa nodded and Hogan left the vardo and went to the gates. Someone cracked them open for him and he slipped inside. Ten minutes later he returned.

'The prof says to invite you and your people into the abbey. We'll open the gates and you can bring your caravans in. Then we shall take a look at the captain.'

Papa bowed. 'Many thanks, American. It is good to see such trust in such dark times.'

'Oh well,' said Hogan. 'I'm a good judge of character.'

'Yes,' agreed Papa. 'And you carry a machine gun, just in case.'

Nathaniel laughed. 'Walk softly and carry a big stick.'

It took over an hour to maneuver all of the

vardos through the stakes and into the quad where they were placed in the traditional circle.

By the time the last vardo was in and the gates closed, Axel had already been placed in the infirmary and a drip was set up supplying him intravenously with Amoxicillin, glucose and pain killers. Janice was thrilled with the huge selection of drugs that the Marine had found and brought back from the hamlet and she and the nurse spent the next hour cataloguing and storing the stock in decent order.

Father O'Hara had introduced himself to Papa Dante and Papa had spread the word that there was a Catholic priest in residence. Although there was no official confession box in the abbey chapel the father had simply erected a board across the part of the knave and already there was a queue of the devoutly Catholic Pavee waiting to confess.

After Papa Dante had finished his confession Nathaniel took him aside.

'Papa,' he said. 'You and your people are most welcome to stay as long as you see fit, however, I must tell you; a child arrived this morning. She had escaped from a village that had been overrun by a large gang, perhaps one hundred and fifty people, who call themselves the Belmarsh Boys. Murderers and rapists. She was lucky to get away alive. She came to warn us that they are coming this way and they mean to take the abbey. Clearly we will resist. This would mean that you and your people would be inadvertently caught in a battle that is not of your making, so, if I were you I would make tracks ASAP in the morning.'

'I have more than twenty men, all armed with automatic weapons.'

Nathaniel nodded.

'If you had not told us then we would have still been here when the gang arrived. Twenty assault rifles would be of great help, would it not?'

'Yes,' agreed the Marine.

'Yet still you warned me and recommended that I leave?'

'I did,' agreed Nathaniel again.

'You weren't tempted to say nothing?'

Nathaniel smiled. 'What do you think?'

Papa Dante put his arm around the Marine's shoulders. 'I think, mister Hogan, that you are a good man. I shall think upon your advice. But tonight, we party.'

'Sounds good,' said the Marine.

And it was good.

Papa's people built a huge bonfire in the center of the quad and laid out tables all round. The prof gave them free access to the abbey stocks of food and alcohol. Bread was baked and vast pots of stew bubbled in cast iron vats, plopping viscously like fragrant witches brews. Bottles of French Cognac were poured into buckets of water to which herbs and sugar had been added to create cocktails that Nathaniel had never tasted before, but were so delicious that he knew that he would have to control his intake. Mama laughed and told him not to worry. The addition of the herbs prevented a hangover, so he could indulge to his heart's content.

Everyone sat around the tables and food was served, alcohol flowed and the conversation levels were high, waves of laughter rippling across the tables.

After everyone had eaten their full, except for father O'Hara who was wolfing down a fourth bowl of stew, the travelers put together a group consisting of a fiddle, a flute and Cajon wooden drum and started to play.

They started with traditional Irish dancing music. Simple drum beat in 4/4 time driven by a racing violin with the flute taking up the melody. Within seconds almost everyone was dancing, twirling and reeling around the fire. The Marine sat and smoked and watched, his face agrin as the outside world sat forgotten for a while behind the stone walls of the abbey.

After almost an hour of dance Mama walked over to the band. She stood in front of them and they stopped playing. She ran her eyes over the crowd, her expression serious but with a hint of a smile.

'This is a traditional song that the Walking People have passed down for many a generation and I would like to sing it now.'

And then she started to sing. Her voice a husky contralto, deep and sensual. The Cajon beat a slow funeral time and the violin dragged out a dirge as the flute played a lilting harmony in a minor key.

Abishai and Bogdan
Donato and Fyodor
From Giannes to Jonetan
Through Michele and Teodor
Abisai unto Zebediah
The beginning and the end
From the Alpha to the Omega
One thing in common do we see
That all these names are just the same
And NATHANIEL do they mean
The name donates a gift from God
A privilege to receive
And with this gift comes power
All for the few and the proud
And glory and duty and a task

To unite the swords of men
In the new time of times gone past
Shout Oorah and Hallelujah
Human kind shall last
And human kind shall last.

Mama bowed and sat down. There was a pause and then everyone applauded. Most did not heed the words but the sheer beauty of the sound brought a sad cheer to the heart. The Marine, however, was less happy. The song was about him. He knew this for certain. It was not about someone named Nathaniel, the coincidences were too many.

Nathaniel had been seconded from Marine Corps Alpha Company into embassy duty. The few and the proud was one of the Marine Corps mottos. And Oorah was the Marine battle cry. Finally, thought the Marine as he stood up, my bloody name is Nathaniel.

He strode across the clearing to Mama who greeted him with a small curtsey.

Nathaniel got straight to the point. 'That song was about me.'

Mama smiled. 'Mayhap,' she said. 'Tis a very old song though. Hundreds of years old. Gogo asked me to sing it.'

Nathaniel had not yet met Gogo. 'Might I speak to her?' He asked.

'Certainly,' said someone behind him.

He turned to see the old woman. Her face was expressionless and her milky eyes danced in the firelight, a mirror of flame and shadow. Almost a Jack-o-lantern. Almost not human.

'Come with me,' she said. 'We shall sit in my vardo and talk.'

The Marine followed her into her caravan and sat down at the table. She poured him a small glass of amber liquid, her movements as assured as someone with full sight.

'Whiskey?' He asked.

'Apple brandy. The very best. We distill it from cider, age it for two years in oak casks. Very powerful,' she saluted the Marine with her glass. 'Slainte!' She knocked it back in one.

Hogan followed suit. It took remarkable self-control not to cough the raw spirit straight back out. It was as rough as oven cleaner and as powerful as aviation fuel. Gogo refilled the glasses, sat back and began to talk.

'That song is called The Few and the Proud,' she said. 'It has been traditional for around three hundred years.'

'So it's not about me than?' Asked Nathaniel.

'Oh, it is about you,' said Gogo. 'It's merely been waiting. And it is merely a tiny part of what you need to know. Firstly, Marine, tell me, what gift have you received?'

Nathaniel pinched the bridge of his nose. 'I seem to be slightly immortal.'

'Slightly immortal?'

'Well, if I get stabbed or, presumably, shot I recover real quick. Even if I should have been dead. As for disease, sickness, starvation, that I don't know.'

'A great gift indeed,' said Gogo. 'Now tell me, soldier, do you know what is happening to the world?'

Nathaniel nodded. 'Some sort of EMP caused by a solar flare or similar. No electrical or electronic items have been left working and, as long as the pulses continue as they are, for the foreseeable future we are basically back in the dark ages.'

'Technically you are correct. However,' continued Gogo. 'There is much more involved in the whole thing. What you see as a simple naturalistic happening or a mere ontological naturalism, we see as a supernatural or even spiritual happening.'

'You mean, end of days, rapture type of thing?' Asked Nathaniel.

Gogo shook her head. 'No. Not an end of days, merely an end of a cycle. The time of technology is at an end. Now is the new time of fascination. Enchantment and glamour.'

'Are you talking about magic?'

Gogo nodded.

'That's ridiculous,' scoffed Nathaniel.

'As ridiculous as suddenly becoming almost immortal?' Countered Gogo.

'Point taken,' admitted the Marine. 'So what are you saying?'

'What I am saying, soldier, is that, no matter how huge you think the past few weeks events have been, they are nothing compared to what the future holds. Now please realize, I speaks from mere feelings, not empirical knowledge, but I have been around for a very long time, Marine, and I tend to be right, more than I am wrong. However, there is one thing that I am completely certain of; you, Nathaniel Hogan, are important. Perhaps even the most important person on the face of the planet. And you have a hard road ahead of you, child. A long and arduous journey that even you with your enhanced powers may not survive. But survive you must for you are our hope. In time you will unite the swords of men, and humankind shall last.'

Nathaniel looked less than happy. 'How, Gogo? And when and where and every bloody question under the sun?'

Gogo laughed. 'I don't have the answers, my child. I do have the feeling that you should continue your journey North but that is only a feeling. Aside from that, Papa Dante tells me that a horde are coming?'

Nathaniel nodded. 'One or two hundred armed thugs. Things are going to get very uncomfortable here.'

'Be that as it may,' said Gogo. 'I have instructed Papa that we will help you defend this place. Use my people, Marine. But use them wisely. And after you have successfully defended the threat then continue on your journey.'

Hogan nodded. 'I will, Gogo.'

'Before you go, child, I want to show you something. And I want you to practice doing this every day. When you can do it with ease then you will know what to do.'

Gogo held up her right hand, palm up. She concentrated on her palm, her breath deep and even. And suddenly a ball of flame, about the size of a golf ball, appeared in the air above her open hand. It bobbed up and down, the flames rolling around. Nathaniel could feel the heat from where he was seated. Then she closed her hand and the flame ceased to exist.

'Wow,' said Nathaniel. 'That's amazing.'

Gogo shook her head. 'No, it's a mere parlor trick. The lowest level of magik. However once you can do that it opens the mind to higher levels. Now, I want you to try to do this every day for at least half an hour. Every day. You will open your hand, concentrate on drawing in energy from all around you and then project that energy into the form of a small ball of fire. It will be the most frustrating thing that you have ever tried to do, but you have the gift. It will come.'

Nathaniel nodded. 'Every day, Gogo. I promise.'

The old lady patted his cheek. 'Good. Now go. Seek bed and rise early, tomorrow we battle evil.'

Nathaniel left the vardo and headed for his room.

Chapter 35

The air shimmered. Fire leapt from stone to stone in the circle of the Merry Maidens in Cornwall. Above the stone circle the Aurora coalesced into a circular rainbow and a shaft of white sunlight burst onto the grass. Lightening sheeted across the heavens, and the sound of thunder rolled over the land, crashing and booming so loudly that the very earth shook. All over England other stones circles shivered in empathy as electrical coronas of light skittered and flashed over them. From Stonehenge to Castlerigg, from Tomnavarie to Bryn Gwyn, the standing stones circles all shimmered with a power that had not been felt for many millennia.

The power of the old magic.

The power of the Life-Light.

And then the fundament tore open to reveal a venereal slit that slowly spread wider and wider.

Through it came the battle Orcs. Running four abreast in full gear, their nostril flaps fluttering as they breathed in and out, two-handed swords drawn and shield to the fore. As they came through they spread out and kept running. The early morning sun picked out their oiled armor and the sharp edges of their blades and painted them a shimmering red.

The column of battle Orcs continued for the next forty-eight hours until almost a quarter of a million battle Orcs had formed a perimeter that covered almost two square miles.

Next came the goblin archers, faster and smaller they came through at a rate of over one hundred an hour, so within another forty hours the full 400 000 of them were through. After that, Ammon ordered the fair folk and their construct retainers through the gateway, confident that, whatever happened, he had 650 000 armed troops on Earth and 560 000 troops protecting the opening of the gateway, including the 10 000 trolls.

By now the Orcs had started to score the surrounding countryside for trees to form stockades, as well as looking for close water supplies and searching out for any danger.

Even though it was a very remote area they were seen by three lots of people. The first; residents of the Bloiegh dairy farm. A mother, father and two sons who took one look at the group of one hundred Orcs stamping towards the farmhouse and simply ran screaming into the wilds of Cornwall.

The second; a group of old farmhands, Cadan Oatey, Perran Penhalligan and Ruan Gluyas. All three were sitting outside the farm's grain storage barn when the group of Orcs came running over the hill. The Orcs stopped and stared at the three old men for a while, deduced that there was neither danger nor wood in their vicinity and carried on.

Ruan Gluyas took his pipe out of his shirt pocket and carefully filled it with a plug of navy shag, tamping it down well with callused, nicotine stained thumb. Then he took out his matches, lit and got the tobacco glowing merrily before he spoke.

'Now that is something that you don't see every day,' he said.

'Wonder what they were?' Asked Cadan.

Ruan shrugged. 'Could be them aliens that you hear talk of.'

Cadan laughed. 'Now surely you don't believe in that shite? Aliens, whatever next?'

'Mind you,' said Perran. 'We did see something and it was something that none of us has seen before and we have all been around for some time now.'

There was a general murmur of agreement. Finally Ruan spoke again. 'Probably some sort of government experiment,' he said.

The two other old men nodded sagely. 'Aye,' agreed Cadan. 'That'll be it, to be sure. Bloody government.'

'First they bugger up our electricity and now they start experimenting with ugly gray pig-men. It's not right, you know. Waste of taxpayers money.'

'When did you ever pay tax?' Asked Cadan.

'That's not the point, is it?' Argued Ruan. 'It's the principle of the thing. If I did pay tax I would be horrified that they was spending my hard earned cash on making gray pig-men.'

Once again there was a general nodding of heads.

'Got any spare baccy?' Asked Cadan.

Ruan handed over his bag.

The Godfrey twins claimed the third sighting. Two brothers who had only recently got out of Wormwood Scrubs after doing a stretch for armed robbery. They had been remanded into their uncle's custody and he had moved them to his run down farm in Cornwall. The two brothers hated the countryside and spent most of their time wandering the fields with a pair of shotguns and decimating the wildlife.

Their reaction upon seeing the group of Orcs was true to form. They simply picked up their shotguns and opened fire. The birdshot bounced off the Orcs thick hides and, while the brothers were busy reloading, the Orc sergeant stepped forward and, with one massive uninterrupted blow, chopped both of the brothers in half, the blade cleaving through them at chest level.

Chapter 36

It was perhaps an hour before sunrise. Nathaniel, Papa Dante, the Prof and father O'Hara stood around a map on a table in the library. Candles provided ample flickering light and the fireplace had a blaze going, filling the room with warmth against the pre-dawn chill.

The Marine was about to start talking when the doors opened and Janice walked in. Ahead of her she was pushing a wheelchair in which sat the injured captain.

Nathaniel immediately stood to rigid attention and saluted.

'Captain.'

Axel saluted back, his movements slow and slightly uncoordinated.

'Master sergeant. At ease, please. No need for that. I know that you are in charge of defense here, I simply wanted to put in my pennies worth. Carry on.'

'Well, sir,' said Nathaniel. 'The first thing that I wanted to discuss is the question of how possible would it be to defend the abbey successfully.'

'How many guns have you got, sergeant?'

'Around twenty plus automatic rifles with Papa Dante's people. The scholars, perhaps twenty shotguns and a few 22 target rifles.'

'So, ten to twelve people per wall?'

Nathaniel nodded.

'Well then, gunney, my informed opinion is, you're well screwed.'

'The walls are good and high, sir. Plus there's a dry moat.'

'They'll come at night,' said Axel. 'First they'll probe. Small groups, in, out fast. A few Molotovs, sniping. Grenades if they've manage to find any. Then they will probably attack in strength in two places at once. I would say the gates and one of the other walls. In the last skirmish that I had with them I would venture to say that we thinned their numbers a little but there are still close to two hundred of them. That means each wall will be receiving anything between seventy and one hundred attackers. They will come with plenty of ladders and will lay down overwhelming firepower. You will take casualties. If you manage to repel them they will do the same again the next night. And the next. Frankly, and I hate to say this, you cannot win.'

There was a pause and then Nathaniel spoke.

'That's pretty much what I suspected, sir. That's why I was going to suggest a different way of looking at the whole thing. I propose that, instead of defending the abbey – we take the fight to them. We lay an ambush and we attack them. That way, we would choose the killing ground and we would be able to concentrate our firepower instead of splitting it between four walls.'

The Marine pointed at the ordnance survey map.

'This is the only route that they can take if they are coming from this village here, where they are currently stationed. Papa will send horse scouts out here and here so that we know when they are coming.' He ran his finger down the track and then stabbed the paper. 'Here. This is where we will destroy them. Note the gradients. Steep inclines on the sides of the road. A perfect pinch-point. Now this is what I want. Papa, get the scouts out ASAP. Secondly, Prof, I need all of the able bodied scholars to come with me to this point on the map. Don't worry, they'll all be safe, I merely need them to help prepare the ambush. We'll need the two wagons we got from the hamlet. Prof, I seem to remember someone saying that there used to be a generator here before the pulse?'

The Prof nodded.

'Diesel or gas?' Asked Nathaniel.

'Diesel.'

'Great. Is there any fuel left?'

Prof nodded. 'Hundreds of liters, actually.'

'Excellent, could you get that loaded onto the wagons along with the scholars, some axes, shovels and picks?'

The Prof nodded.

'Okay,' continued the Marine. 'I am going to use Papa Dante's people and myself in the ambush. The scholars, under the Prof and father O'Hara, will stay here as a second line of defense in case any of the horde get through. Oorah, gentlemen.'

There was silence.

Nathaniel raised his voice. 'I said, 'Oorah!'

Everyone shouted at once and the windows rattled so loud was the cry.

'Oorah!'

Chapter 37

Marine master sergeant Nathaniel Hogan stood in the middle of the road. He wore full battle armor. Even the ceramic plates and helmet. He had linked all of his machine gun ammunition together and wound the one long belt around his shoulders. His Colt was on his left hip with two more full magazines. On his right hip was the double-headed war axe. At his feet, two Molotov cocktails. It was the late afternoon of that same day. He had an unlit cigarette in his mouth.

And around the corner came the Belmarsh Boys. Jonathan Naybor rode in sartorial elegance on top of the horse drawn Jaguar. Next to him were his bodyguards on horse. And behind him, ten abreast, were another one hundred and seventy rapists, thieves and murderers. He saw the lone soldier standing in the road and he held his hand up to indicate a halt. Behind him his cohorts lurched to a ragged stop.

'Who are you?' Shouted Naybor.

Nathaniel ignored him. Took out his Zippo. Lit his cigarette. Dragged. Exhaled.

'I asked who you are.' Shouted Naybor once again.

Nathaniel lent down, picked up the two Molotovs, lit them and threw them overhand, one on each side of the road. The flaming bottles arced high into the sky and then came crashing down into the brush on the sides of the road. At the top of the incline that hemmed the road in. Exactly where Nathaniel and the scholars had spent the afternoon piling up a six-foot high line of dry brush and covering it with diesel and gasoline. The side of the road literally exploded with flame trapping the Belmarsh boys in the depression.

At the same time, Papa Dante and his men opened up from behind the Belmarsh boys, automatic weapons pouring a wall of lead into the criminal gang.

This meant that the horde had only one way to go. And that was forward. Naybor couldn't believe his luck. He had been ambushed by the world's worst tactician. A perfect trap except for the fact that the only way to get out of it was through a single man. It was ludicrous.

He raised his hand above his head and brought it chopping down.

'Charge!'

Nathaniel dropped his cigarette, rose up onto the balls of his feet, and sprinted straight at the enemy. At the same time some of Papa's men started to kick bundles of the burning brush down into the road. The balls of flaming kindling rolled into the crowd of thugs, exploding on contact, causing tens of them to catch alight as they crashed into one another in an attempt to escape the flames. Burning people dropped to the ground and rolled, screaming in agony as they burned to death. The extra ammunition that they were carrying cooked off in the flames, exploding and adding to the complete chaos and mayhem.

And then Nathaniel opened up, working the SAW machinegun from side to side. Spent brass poured out of the side of the weapon like metal confetti at a wedding. The high velocity full metal jacket rounds tore through the pack of humanity, sometimes exiting one body only to go on and hit a second and sometimes even a third.

Nathaniel's ammunition lasted for twenty-eight seconds. In that short time he killed over ninety Belmarsh boys. Another ten had succumbed to fire and Papa's men had taken out a further twenty.

The Marine slowed to a walk, dropped the machine gun and pulled out his Colt, firing as he walked. Every shot was a hit. As he fired the last round in his final magazine his luck ran out.

Although he had been hit three or four times the body armor had deflected the shots. But this round, fired from a heavy caliber handgun, struck him under the armor, just above his hip. The round smashed his liver and kidneys and stopped against his spine.

Nathaniel ripped the axe from his belt and beheaded the person who had shot him. Another shot hit him in the right thigh and he staggered but pulled himself upright. The surviving fifty of the Belmarsh boys rushed forward to pack around him but Papa Dante and his boys were still firing, picking their shots with deadly accuracy. Half of the pack turned to face Papa Dante and the others continued to bear down on Nathaniel.

Nathaniel looked at them and smiled. He closed his eyes for a second and felt the power rush into him. Heat boiled off him and time slowed down. Milliseconds became seconds; seconds became minutes and minutes stretched out for days into the future. For he was Nathaniel Hogan and he had been gifted.

The axe flew in his hands, its heavy metal blades as light as gossamer and as deadly as sin as he carved his way through the crowd. Body parts leapt from their owners and rib cages shattered and brains spilt. Such carnage had not been seen since Samson slew a thousand men with the jawbone of a donkey.

Finally the Marine stood in front of Naybor, the commander of the now extinct Belmarsh boys.

'Who are you?' Naybor asked for a final time, his voice shaking with fear.

'I am Marine Master Sergeant Nathaniel Hogan,' was the answer as the axe swept down from on high and clove the commander in twain.

'And I am…THE FOREVER MAN!'

Please look for the next book in the series…

The Forever Man
Book 2: Axeman

Here is a sample to check out –

Chapter 1 Book 2

Toilet paper. Twin ply. Super soft.

Nathaniel grinned to himself.

And coffee. Made with a machine. By a barista. Strong, bitter, honest to God coffee.

Thousands of years of human endeavor. Countless millions of man-hours of invention had been wiped out by the pulse. Computers. Space travel. Brain surgery. And what did the forever man miss the most? Something soft to wipe his ass with and a mildly addictive hot beverage made from the roasted seeds of the Rubiaceae bush.

Nathaniel's horse stumbled slightly. Weary from the days riding. Snow crunched like broken glass beneath its hooves. The air resonant with the fragrance of pine resin and ozone overlaid by the subtle steel smell of newly minted snow. Gusts of wind shivered the trees, shaking clumps of white from their laden boughs. A giant baker dusting the land with icing sugar. Breath steamed from Nate's open mouth in clouds of condensate, leeching the warmth from his core. Puff the magic dragon.

Winter had come across the land with a speed that baffled all. And it was the harshest winter in living memory. Nathaniel had heard theories that the unprecedented level of cold was brought about by the fact that there were no longer any factories left in the world. Nor heating of any sort. The cattle population had been decimated and there were no cars to fill the atmosphere with carbon monoxide. Global cooling had become a reality.

It had been about three months now since the first electromagnetic pulse had struck the earth. Destroying all electronic and electrical equipment in an orgy of solar destruction. And the pulses had continued on a daily basis, apparent by the almost constant glow of the Aurora Borealis, or Northern lights, in the sky that was caused by the massive amounts of gamma radiation in the atmosphere.

But, apart from smashing mankind back into the dark ages, the gamma rays had also had another effect. Somehow they had changed Marine master sergeant Nathaniel Hogan's

DNA structure. They had enhanced his speed, strength and, most of all, his ability to heal. He was now capable of sustaining fatal wounds and recovering. Although, he was still able to succumb to normal disease and starvation. He wasn't sure about drowning. Unfortunately he still felt pain. And normal common garden fatigue. But then one doesn't look an immortal horse in the mouth.

Nathaniel glanced down at the back of his left hand. The pink scar stood out like a brand.

∞

He had dreamed of Stonehenge and druids one night and one of the druids had cut the symbol into his hand with a sickle. When he had awoken it was there. An ancient Traveling women had told him that it was the sign for Infinity and he had been marked as The Forever Man. And then she had shown him some a small magik trick. Conjuring up fire with though alone. She had told him to practice this every day as he had the gift. He had been doing so for almost two months now but to no avail. If the entire world hadn't become so topsy-turvy he would have dismissed her as a weirdo but given the current circumstances he was loath to do so. She had also instructed him to go north to seek his destiny. This he was doing. And, in lieu of any other plan, he was happy to do.

The Marine decided to stop for the night and looked around for a likely spot, finally deciding on a fallen tree a little way off the beaten track. He hitched his horse to a tree, took out his collapsible shovel from one of the saddlebags and started to clear a spot next to the fallen tree, shoveling the snow aside and forming a low three foot wall in a horseshoe shape. When he had finished he spread a tarpaulin on the ground and then a couple of fur blankets. The blankets were black mink, as was the cloak that Nathaniel was wearing. He had come across a specialist fur shop in one of the small towns that he had traveled through and he had helped himself to a half a dozen black minks. Then, with clumsy male stitching, he had converted two of the coats into a full-length cloak. The other four had become two separate blankets. It amused him that his little bivouac now contained over one hundred thousand dollars worth of fur at pre-pulse prices.

He spread another tarpaulin over the walls to make a low roof. Then he collected wood and kindling and built a small fire close to the entrance. The fire would keep the shelter warm and keep predators from coming inside. After that, before the light went, he placed five rabbit snares in likely looking places. Finally he took three skinned and dressed squirrels from his saddle bags, spitted them and placed them over the fire to cook whilst he took the saddle off the horse and rubbed it down before putting a blanket over it.

After he had eaten, Nathaniel fell into a deep and restful sleep. He awoke the next morning about half an hour before sunrise, stoked the fire and went to check the traps. Two had been successful and he took the rabbits back and skinned and gutted them. For breakfast he threw a couple of old potatoes into the fire and then he melted some snow in a pot for drinking water.

Finally he packed up, got back into the saddle and continued on his unplanned way.

As the day wore on he started to pass more and more houses. He stopped to check a few but they were mostly empty. And those that were not empty contained only corpses. The lack of food, drugs and heating had taken a massive toll on the survivors of the initial pulse and now, a mere three months on, Nathaniel estimated that a full fifty percent of the population were dead. Over thirty million people.

Even so, he had expected to find some people in the houses. But the area was dead. Totally devoid of humanity.

Late that afternoon he came across the reason why. According to his map he was standing outside the rural village of Acton-on-vale. But what he saw in front of him looked nothing like a rural village. Running left to right the entire area was fenced in with steel reinforced concrete blast panels. Three meters high. Every one hundred yards a scaffold observation post rose another meter above the fence. Each observation post contained a soldier armed with a light machine gun. Far to his right he could see a steel gate. The gate was open and five armed guards stood in front of it. They were dressed in MTP camouflage and carried the SA80Mk3 assault rifles. One of them was already walking towards Nathaniel, his weapon brought to bear.

Nate dismounted and walked slowly towards the soldier, one hand on the horse's reins and the other held up above his head.

The approaching soldier seemed satisfied that Nate meant no harm and he lowered his rifle.

'Can I help?' He asked.

'Just passing through, lance corporal. Stopped to admire your wall.'

'You're welcome to come inside and take a look,' said the soldier. 'All are welcome as long as they obey then rules.' The soldier stared at Nathaniel for a moment and then asked. 'Is that a military uniform under your cloak?'

Nathaniel nodded. 'Master sergeant Nathaniel Hogan, United States Marine Corps.'

'The soldier came to attention, shouldering his rifle. 'Pleased to meet you, sir. I wonder if I might insist that you accompany me inside, sir. The Brigadier has ordered that all military personnel be introduced to him before they go on their way.'

Nate shrugged. 'Lead the way, Lance

corporal.'

Nathaniel led his horse and followed the lance corporal to the gate. When he got there two of the soldiers barred his way.

'Sorry, sir,' said the one. 'You need to check in all weapons before you go inside. We'll keep them safe and issue you with a ticket. Also, we'll take care of your horse. No horses allowed inside the perimeter.'

'Fair enough,' conceded Nate. He pulled back his cloak and unholstered two sawn-off double-barreled shotguns that rode in hip holsters. Then he unsheathed a rifle from the horse's saddle. Finally he removed his double-headed battle-axe from the loop in his belt and handed it to one of the soldiers, then he hitched back his cloak so that it hung down his back, exposing his rank flashes. The soldier raised his one eyebrow but refrained from comment.

They wrote a receipt out in a small carbon book and gave Nate a copy.

'With me, sir,' said the lance corporal.

Nate followed him as he walked through the open gates and headed towards the center of the village. He saw a few soldiers walking around and one or two civilians but on the whole, the place seemed remarkably empty.

'Where is everyone?' He asked.

'Working,' answered the lance corporal.

'Where?'

The soldier didn't answer and Nate couldn't be bothered to push him. He would ask the Brigadier.

Eventually they came to a massive Victorian rectory. Two armed men stood at attention outside the front door.

Nate and the lance corporal mounted the stairs.

'Someone to see the brigadier,' said the lance.

The guards waved him through. The lance opened the front door and ushered Nate in, closing it behind him.

The entrance hall was huge, Persian carpets were scattered across the mahogany floor, large oils of landscapes and horses lined the walls. A fire crackled in the walk in fireplace and the light from thirty or more candles reflected off the stupendous crystal chandelier.

The lance carried on through the hall and down a corridor, stopping at the second door and knocking twice.

Within seconds the door was opened by a tall, stooped, gray haired man sporting the uniform and flashes of a warrant officer class 1.

'Visitor for the brigadier, sir,' announced the lance.

The warrant officer nodded. 'Thank your,

lance corporal. I'll take it from here.'

The lance swiveled on his heel and left.

The warrant officer waved Nate into the room.

Nathaniel marched into the center of the room and came crashing to attention in front of the warrant officer and the brigadier. A short, wide man with cropped black hair and bristle moustache. He was dressed in combat uniform with his rank slide on his chest as opposed to shoulder badges. On his hip a Glock 17.

The Marine whipped up a solid parade ground salute, stood at rigid attention and bellowed in his best master sergeant voice.

'Marine corps master sergeant Nathaniel Hogan reporting as requested, sir.'

The brigadier's face registered his approval. 'At ease, mister Hogan.'

Nathaniel raised his right knee parallel to the floor and slammed it down as he shifted to the 'at ease' position, hands behind his back, thumbs interlocked, left in front of right.

'Stand easy, mister Hogan,' continued the brigadier.

Nathaniel relaxed almost imperceptibly apart from the fact that he now looked at the brigadier as opposed to straight ahead.

'So, soldier, what brings you here?' Asked the Brigadier.

'Simply passing through, sir.'

'We're looking for more soldiers, particularly non-comms. Could we interest you in staying?'

'With respect, sir,' answered Nate. 'I would prefer to continue my journey.'

The Brigadier nodded. 'Fine, but I insist that you stay as our guest for two or three days. Take a look around, see what we're all about. Mayhap I can change your mind. Mister Clarkson here will show you to your quarters and issue you with the necessaries.'

Nate crashed to attention once more. 'Thank you, sir. Much appreciated.' He saluted again and followed warrant officer Clarkson out of the room.

Clarkson led him to the next room and ushered him in. He went over to a desk and pulled out a sheaf of papers, signed a few and handed them to Nate.

'Here you go, mister Hogan These are permission slips. The yellow ones are for a day's accommodation, I have given you three. The green ones are for food. One meal per slip. I have allowed you two meals a day, breakfast and supper. Come with me and I'll show you to your digs.'

Nate followed Clarkson out of the house,

past the armed guards and down the road. Once again it struck Nate that there were next to no civilians present. He didn't bother to ask Clarkson where they were, figuring that he would find out later.

The snow had been cleared from all of the roads and pavements and there was no litter. Even the street signs had been cleaned and polished. All of these obvious pointers to the fact that the village was being militarily run.

After a few turns they came to a small Victorian terraced cottage. Clarkson opened the front door, which was unlocked and showed Nate in.

'Here you go, old chap. The water is running, we've set up a gravity feed tower, cold but drinkable and fine for washing in if you're a complete Spartan. Please feel free to wander. If you'd like to go outside the perimeter one has to get permission from the Brigadier, I'm afraid. The officers mess in the village hall, sure that you can find that by yourself. Any questions?'

Nate shook his head. 'No, sir. All self-evident. Many thanks. Oh, maybe one, what about my horse?'

'Shouldn't worry about that, mister Hogan. The chaps will take good care of it.'

The warrant officer left, closing the door behind him as he did.

Nate took a walk through of the cottage. Two rooms downstairs, a sitting room and a kitchen. Off the kitchen was a small shower room and toilet. A stiff towel was hanging over the rail.

Narrow stairs to the first floor. At the top another two small rooms. Both rooms contained double beds. On the one bed was a set of linen. Sheets, a blanket, single thin pillow and a duvet. There were no personal items to be seen and Nate wondered what had happened to the previous inhabitants.

Nate decided to take a shower first. He stripped down in the bedroom and laid his clothes out on the bed. His spare clothes were in his saddlebags on his horse so he would have to make do for the meanwhile.

Naked he walked down stairs, went into the bathroom and turned the shower on. The water was ice cold, only a little above freezing but Nate stepped in, grabbed the sliver of soap and, puffing and blowing, scrubbed himself down and rinsed off. He rubbed himself dry with the rough towel and jogged back up to the bedroom to get dressed, pulling his mink coat tight around his shoulders until he had warmed up. Then he strapped on his boots and went outside.

He simply started to meander about the village without any special purpose. After a couple of turns he came across a large military tent pitched in a front garden. Steam billowed out of the side of the canvas structure and a strange smell of vinegar and sugar and fruit wafted through the air. He walked over to the open front of the tent to take a look. A single armed guard stood in the entrance. When he saw Nate he nodded, obviously aware that he was around, but he said nothing.

Nate peered in to see a long row of villagers working over large catering pots that were suspended above cooking fires. Opposite them were another group of people working at a preparation table, slicing vegetables, peeling fruit, measuring and weighing. It didn't take Nate long to realize that they were pickling vegetables and turning fruit into preserves for the winter. Planning ahead. Everyone had their heads down, working hard, so he didn't talk to anyone. He simply watched for a short while and went on his way.

On the outskirts of the village in what looked like a horse paddock, he saw a large group of children, eight years to around twelve, marching around the arena. Instead of rifles they carried tools. Spades, garden forks, picks and shovels. A corporal called out time, berating those who fell out of step and complimenting those who marched straight and proud. The children wore khaki shirts and trousers and each had a square badge on their chest. A flag with a red cross of St. George and a sun and a moon in the top corners. On their right sleeves a small rectangular flash of white with the words, "The needs of the many outweigh the needs of the few".

The sight sent a shiver through Nate as memories of school history lessons and photo's of rows of Hitler Youth Children flashed through his mind.

The corporal saw Nate watching and beckoned to him to come over.

'Greetings, Master Sergeant,' he said. 'Taking a look at out budding troops, I see.'

Nate nodded. 'Very impressive. Do they learn to shoot?'

'Oh yes. Field craft, weapon craft, doctrine, fitness, survival training. The Brigadier says that these are the future of our new world.'

'When do they get time for schooling?'

'They receive rudimentary reading, writing and arithmetic skills. The Brigadier believes that too much focus on intellectual pursuits will be damaging to their development as soldiers. Some of the more feeble ones, ones of less physical strength, are selected for more cerebral offerings.'

Nate kept his face devoid of expression and simply nodded and went on his way.

Next he came across a group of four civilians, a man and three women of indeterminate middle age. Standing near them was an armed soldier. Two of the women were sweeping the snow off the roads and sidewalks and the other two were polishing the road signs. The soldier nodded a greeting but the civilians kept their eyes downcast and avoided looking at him as they concentrated on their menial tasks. As Nate drew away he heard one of them coughing, a deep wracking cough that sounded like the precursor of real problems.

Nate continued his aimless stroll, noting that all of the sidewalks and roads were clear of snow, the signs all polished and the fences newly painted. The village was in parade ground condition. No longer a village and now an obvious military base. Once again he wondered where all of the inhabitants were.

He walked alongside the blast wall until he came to one of the sentry towers. It stood four meters high and was constructed from steel scaffolding. A ladder ran up the side to the platform.

Nate gave the sentry a shout. 'Hey, soldier. Mind if I come up?'

The soldier peered over the side, took in Nate's rank and gave a thumbs up. 'Help yourself, sir.'

Nate shimmied up the ladder and stepped onto the platform. The area was around six square yards, three-foot high railings and a 7.62 mm machine gun mounted on a swing mount that was attached to a steel stanchion.

The Marine nodded to the soldier. 'Nathaniel Hogan, Marine master sergeant.'

'Private Johnson, sir. Surrey territorials.'

Nate pulled out a pack of cigarettes and offered. Johnson accepted with alacrity, a huge grin on his face.

'Thank you, sir. Ran out of these over a month ago. Commissioned officers only.'

Nate lit for both of them and then gave the rest of the pack to the private.

'Here, take them. I've got more.'

Johnson slipped the pack into one of the pouches of his webbing, his face still agrin.

The two soldiers smoked in silence for a while and Nate surveyed the land. About six hundred yards from the rear wall he could see a group of people working in a field, scraping the snow to one side and digging up something that looked like potatoes. Three armed guards stood close by them. He also noticed small groups walking through the forest. Groups of threes and fours. Each with a soldier.

'What are they doing?' He asked Johnson.

'Laying traps, sir. Rabbits, birds, small game. The meat is brought back and either used straightaway or smoked and salted for storage. Also general forage, wild carrots, tubers, fruits. The Brigadier has set up a system. We need to be fully self sustaining ASAP. No relying on old generation tinned foods and such, sir. We are the new generation.'

Nate dragged on his cigarette. Said nothing.

'These people owe a lot to the Brigadier,' continued Johnson. 'We were on exercises in the area, using the local base, only a couple of hundred of us. The bulk of the boys were in Afghanistan when the power went. Within a day the Brigadier had a plan, reckoned that the base was indefensible as well as being unsustainable. So we decamped to this village. If it weren't for us it they would all have starved. Now we have food being stored for the winter, running water, defenses. The continuation of our civilization. And it won't stop here. In time we can expand, bring more people under rule. Make more people safe.'

Nate nodded. Whatever he thought, it was obvious that the Brigadier had achieved a great deal in a small amount of time.

'Right then,' he said to Johnson. 'Thanks for the info. See you later.'

He climbed back down the tower and continued his circuit of the wall finally ending up at the village green.

There was a large army tent erected in the middle of the green and he could see through the entrance that it was full of trestle tables and a variety of chairs. Most of the tables were full of people sitting down and eating and there were still long queues at the chow line as people waited patiently, bowls in hand, to get some sustenance.

Nate could smell the food from where he stood and it seemed to consist mainly of boiled turnips, potato and cabbage. Way in the background a slight smell of meat. Probably rabbit. The villagers looked lethargic, faces pale and movements slow. Whenever he caught someone's eye they immediately looked down, their faces showing obvious fear.

The Marine contemplated missing dinner as the smell of the turnips was turning his stomach but he hadn't eaten since that morning so he figured that he had better try to get something into his belly while he had the chance.

He continued past the green to the village hall where Clarkson had told him the officers mess was. The front doors were closed and he let himself in. The first thing that struck him was the atmosphere. Someone, a young girl it seemed, was playing a piano in the corner. Classical renditions of pop songs. The place was well lit with candles and mirrors and a fire crackled away in the hearth, filling the place with warmth. And the smell of the food immediately made his mouth water.

Fried chicken, mashed potato with butter, peas, gravy, corn. There were bottles of red wine at the tables as well as jugs of water and fresh fruit juice. It was as if he had entered another world. A world of privilege and power. And then he realized; that is exactly what he had done. Outside were the new world peasants. The grubbers of dirt and the wielders of plows. And in this room were the leaders of the elite. Soldiers. Warriors. Men with power.

Nathaniel took a deep breath and walked into the room.

The brigadier, who was sitting at the top table, saw him and beckoned to him.

'Mister Hogan. Join us.'

Nate walked over and sat down next to the commanding officer.

'So, mister Hogan,' continued the Brigadier. 'You've had a good look around. What do you think.'

'I'm a sergeant, sir,' responded Nate. 'Not my job to think.'

The Brigadier smiled. But only with his lips, no humor touched his eyes. 'I give you permission to think. Go ahead.'

'Very efficiently run outfit, sir,' said Nate. 'Not sure if I'd want to be a civilian.'

The brigadier raised an eyebrow. 'Why?'

'Well, sir, never been one for grubbing in the dirt and surviving on turnip soup.'

The brigadier nodded. 'I see. You appear to have come across the lower echelons being fed. The tent on the green. Yes,' agreed the brigadier. 'It's a tough life for them. However, better than being dead one might say. But what you do not know, mister Hogan, is those were only a part of the community. The lowest and least skilled of the village. There is another kitchen closer to the gates where the middle echelons are fed. Those are the people with more discernable skills. Blacksmiths, engineers, farmers, farriers and such. Their fare is substantially better than turnip soup.'

'As good as this?' Asked Nate.

The brigadier laughed. 'Of course not. We are officers. The enlisted men get similar food, no booze. But the middle echelons get a meat ration and bread with their soup. An adequate amount of calories to survive and to work.'

'There seem to be many empty houses, sir. Casualties?'

'No,' answered the brigadier. 'Thanks to us there were very few casualties in the village. We've had, perhaps, a ten percent die back. Diabetics, people whom were on various life giving drugs that ran out, the elderly. The empty houses are part of the new order. One is assigned housing depending on ones usefulness to the community as a whole. The lower echelons share housing. Four to a room, male and females separated. The middles echelons get their own house, ranging from a three bedroom for the farrier down to smaller one or two beds for farmers and assistants. The doctor has a very decent digs as does the priest.'

'As do you, sir,' interjected Nate.

'Yes, I am the commanding officer. My place used to belong to a city trader. Now he is one of the lower echelons. Good for nothing but wielding a spade. No discernable skills whatsoever.'

'And what are the empty houses for then?' Enquired the Marine.

'Newcomers, such as yourself,' said the brigadier. 'We accept all comers, interview them, allocate them a job and in return they get food, shelter and safety.'

Someone put a full plate of food down in front of Nate and he concentrated on getting it inside him. The brigadier sat silently for a while, sipping on a glass of red wine. After a minute or so he stood up. Immediately everyone in the room stood to attention.

The brigadier waved them back down. 'As you were, gentlemen. I grow weary and shall take my leave.' He left the hall followed closely by his two armed guards and everyone sat down and continued with their meals.

Warrant officer Clarkson, who was sitting on Nate's left side, offered the Marine a glass of wine. Nate nodded his thanks.

'He's a great man, you know,' said Clarkson. 'What you see is just the beginning. Soon we shall start to expand our net. Bring in more villages and towns under us, set up communications via fast horse. Expand the central army to include a militia. Create centralized farms and production units. Everyone will have equal access to food and shelter.'

'Except for the military,' rejoined Nathaniel.

'Well, obviously, yes. For any civilization to achieve, one must have a ruling class.'

Nate said nothing.

'You seem skeptical, master sergeant.'

'I don't know if skeptical is the correct word,' answered Nathaniel. 'Perhaps incredulous is closer.'

'Why?'

'Military rule? Armies are run to fight wars, not to rule civilizations. Look at Hitler, Adi Amin, Stalin, Genghis Kahn. Power can be gained by the barrel of a gun but never held.'

'You misunderstand, master sergeant. We do not seek to conquer. We seek to help. We have no political agenda at all.'

'War is the continuation of politics,' argued Nate. 'And before you say that you aren't at war let me tell you – you are. What would happen if you stood your soldiers down and disarmed them?'

'Obviously there might be a breakdown of discipline,' admitted Clarkson.

Nate snorted. 'A breakdown of discipline? The people would rise up and slaughter the lot of you.'

Clarkson shook his head vehemently. 'No way, master sergeant. They understand that what we are doing is for the best. The needs of the many outweigh the needs of the few. As I say, a few may become a little undisciplined but not much more.'

'Bullshine,' said Nate. 'They won't even look a soldier in the eye. They're all living in terror. While you have taken their houses and split up their families and dine on fried chicken whilst they subsist on turnip water. Wake up, man.'

Clarkson had gone pale with rage as he stared at Nate. 'Master sergeant,' he said. 'You are dismissed. You are no longer welcome in the officer's mess. Please leave this instant.'

Nathaniel stood up. 'I'm sorry, mister Clarkson. I didn't mean to offend. Especially after being given such a welcome. It was churlish of me in the extreme. I shall leave first thing in the morning after extending my thanks to the Brigadier.'

Nate bowed and walked slowly from the hall and into the night. A light snow was falling; little eddies of wind causing it to swirl about the Marine's head like moths around a flame.

He took out a cigarette, cupped his hands against the wind and lit up. Then he walked back to his digs, deep in thought. He didn't know why he was so riled up. Most of what Clarkson said was true; the bulk of the villagers would have died by now if left to their own devices. The brigadier had created a safe haven in a world gone mental. The bulk of the villagers were eating, albeit subsistence rations. But the whole thing stank like a nine-day-old kipper. Sometimes, just because you could do something, was no real reason to go ahead and do it. One thing was for sure; the brigadier was on one huge power trip. Nevertheless, thought Nate, whilst the situation was not to his liking it wasn't actually broken. People were safe and alive, far be it for him to blunder in righting wrongs that were not even considered wrongs by many of the people involved.

He arrived at his digs and stood outside for a while, dragging on the remains of his cigarette. As he finished, the door of the cottage three down from his crashed open and two soldiers stepped out. Between them was a young girl. Perhaps fifteen or maybe sixteen. It was hard to tell in the dark but it looked as if she had been weeping. Behind her was an older man, gray hair, spectacles.

'You can't do this,' the older man said. His voice a desperate plea.

'Brigadier's orders,' replied the one soldier. 'Now stand back.'

The older man lunged forward and grabbed the girl, attempting to pull her from the soldier's grasp. The soldier who had spoken before, casually smashed his elbow into the man's face, splitting the flesh below his eye and knocking him to the ground, sending his spectacles flying.

Nate strode over. 'What's going on here?' He asked.

'Back off, 'retorted the soldier.

'Back off – sergeant,' bellowed Nate.

The soldier came to attention. 'Sorry, sergeant,' he said. 'My mistake. Thought that you were a civvie. Brigadier's orders, sergeant. He said to bring the girl to his offices.'

'Why?' Asked Nate.

The private shrugged. 'Not mine to ask, sergeant. Not in this man's army. Brigadier commands and I do.'

Nathaniel nodded. It was the answer that he expected. A private was a mere pawn in an institution where shit ran downhill so he was constantly covered in the stuff. Every crappy job went to the lowest ranks first.

'As you were, private,' said Nate. 'Just make sure that no harm comes to the girl.'

Once again the private shrugged. 'It will or it won't, sergeant, but I can assure you, I will not harm her.'

The two soldiers dragged the weeping girl off.

Nate picked up the older man's spectacles and handed them to him.

The man accepted them with shaking hand. 'How could you?' He said. 'She's but a child. She's my granddaughter. Barely fifteen years old.'

'I'm sure that she'll be fine,' replied Nate.

The old man shook his head. 'I know that you've just got here, but how can you be so naïve? What do you think is happening here? Do you think that monster has invited her over for milk and cookies?'

Nate turned and started to walk back to his digs.

The old man grabbed his cloak. 'He's going to rape her. He's going to take my little girl and tear her clothes off and beat her and rape her.' He started to weep. Quietly. Then he let go of Nate's cloak and simply sat down in the snow, tears running down his cheeks. 'He's going to rape her and there's nothing that I can do.'

Nate stood and watched him for a while. Thoughts tumbled through his mind. The needs of then many outweigh the needs of the few. These people had shelter. Food. Protection from the roving gangs. But who would protect them from their protectors? And why should it be his problem? He would go back to his house, sleep, get up tomorrow and go. Leave well enough alone.

The old man held his head in his hands and rocked back and forth slightly. A picture of utter dejection.

'Oh stuff it,' said Nate,' as he turned and started to stride towards the brigadier's house. 'I know that I'm going to regret this.'

It took him less than two minutes to reach the brigadier's house and he walked straight up to the front door. The two ever-present guards blocked his way.

'Sorry, sergeant,' said the one. 'No entrance. The brigadier is busy for the evening.'

'No,' said Nate. 'Not any more.' He grabbed the guard's rifle and pulled the man towards him, arching his back and delivering a crashing head butt to the bridge of the man's nose. He dropped to the floor like a sack of wheat. Nate ripped the rifle from his inert fingers, swung on his heel and smacked the butt into the other guard's temple, dropping him in the same manner.

Then he opened the door ands walked in. He figured that the brigadier would be upstairs and he ran up the sweeping marble staircase to the next floor. He entered a corridor with a row of doors along one side and a set of double doors at the very end. Nate reckoned that the double doors were probably the entrance to the master suit so he went straight to them and kicked them open.

The girl was naked and tied to the bed. The brigadier, still in full dress uniform, stood over her with a riding crop. The red swollen weals that criss-crossed the girl's torso spoke of mute testament as to what the brigadier was doing.

He turned to face Nate, his face a picture of absolute surprise.

'What the bloody hell?' He exclaimed. 'How dare you, sergeant? Get out.'

Nate raised the rifle and pointed it at the brigadier. 'You filthy old animal, put the whip down and untie the girl.'

The brigadier's face went purple with rage. 'Put the rifle down this instant. You are addressing a superior officer.'

'No I'm not,' said Nate. 'I'm merely addressing an officer that outranks me. Now do as I say or I swear that I'll shoot your dick off.'

But the brigadiers could still not get past the enormity of being addressed in such a way by a mere non-commissioned officer, so he simply shook his head and shouted, 'guards!'

Nate, who was not one to issue idle threats, flicked the safety off the rifle and fired a round into the floor next to the officer's feet. 'Untie her, or the next one will leave you singing soprano for the rest of your life.'

The officer stepped over to the bed and quickly untied the girl.

'Where are her clothes?' Asked Nate.

The brigadier pointed to a pile in the corner.

'Get dressed, sweetheart,' said Nate. 'What's your name?'

'Stacey,' she replied. Her voice shaking.

Okay, Stacey, quickly now, get dressed and then come and stand by me.'

The girl did as she was told and then stood behind Nate.

'What now?' She asked.

'Damned if I know, Stacey.' answered Nate. 'I'm making this up as I go along.' He used his rifle to motion towards the door. 'Come on, brigadier. Outside, you first.'

The brigadier opened the door and walked out. Nate followed and, as he stepped out into the corridor, a sixth sense told him to move. He stared to pull back but it was too late. A rifle butt smashed into his cheek, splitting the skin and knocking him down. Immediately a veritable herd of boots started kicking him. At least five men, crowding in close and giving it all that they had. He felt his nose break with a gravel-like crunch. Then he distinctly heard at least three ribs and a collarbone break. Dry dull snapping sounds.

Just before he passed out he found just enough time to berate himself for being such an idiot.

****

Hi guys and thanks for giving The Forever Man a go. If you enjoyed it please could you take a bit of time to leave a review, I would really appreciate it!

The rest of the "Forever Man" books are available from Amazon – below are the links…

The Forever Man – Book 2
https://amzn.com/B00L4IA9EO
The Forever Man – Book 3
https://amzn.com/B00NRD0P84
The Forever Man – Book 4
https://amzn.com/B00SW6YHEE
The Forever Man – Book 5
https://amzn.com/B00YUY4YD6
The Forever Man – Book 6
https://amzn.com/B01DJLYEMG

If you would like to be kept in the loop regarding when my next book is out or if you would simply like to email and have a chat please drop me a line at zuffs@sky.com

This is my private email and I will get straight back to you.

Cheers - Craig

PS You may want to give my Shadowhunter series a go.

Emily Shadowhunter – Vampire Killer.

Printed in Great Britain
by Amazon